A PROUD LITTLE TOWN

First in the occasional Arlington Town series

A Novel

by

Eugenie Rounds Rayner

A Proud Little Town is a work of fiction. Names, characters, places, and incidents either are the product of the author's imagination or are used fictitiously. Any resemblance to actual persons, living or dead, events or locales, is entirely coincidental.

Branch Hill Publications, Bennington, Vermont.

ISBN-13: 978-0692705940

ISBN-10: 0692705945

Table of Contents

This book is dedicated to the late Leslie Williams, my writing mentor and writing companion while I was at Vermont College. Leslie encouraged me to make what had been a short story into the work that turned into my first novel. I think she'd be pleased that I had a second novel in me, and, it seems, even a third.

She'd be tickled, too, that I have passed on to numerous others her suggestion to add coffee grounds to brownie mixes. She made a big difference in my life in many ways, not just writing and brownies, and I will always hold her dear in my heart.

"There is a sense in which we are all each other's consequences."

Wallace Stegner

ALL THE LITTLE LIVE THINGS

Chapter One

Town Meeting Day

No one knew it yet, but the bones were lying just a few inches below the surface of the snow that blanketed the banks of the Battenkill River and Lye Brook. A few warmer days and the resulting frost heaves would gradually unearth them. Unless it snowed again.

***

Matthew Spencer was not looking forward to tomorrow. He didn't relish the drive up to Vermont, for one thing, but he had work he wanted to do – he needed to do – and he just wanted that damn meeting out of the way so he could get on with it.

Tomorrow was too important to mess up anything, so Spencer spent Monday night on the phone with his two associates. He read them his notes to help them finish their preparations in time for the three of them to go over everything yet again before the meeting started.

Spencer reminded his colleagues they had to be careful around the eminent domain issue. He knew he was skirting a legality or two, but his associates didn't seem to know that, or it didn't matter to them, so he tried to make sure they were the ones to use the phrase. The two words alone were enough to scare people, and he didn't want to be the one people associated with the concept.

Town Meeting Day dawned cold and sunny, and Abby Phillips, MD, pulled on her thick parka and rubber boots as she prepared to go outside to brush off the night's snow from the old Subaru. Her plan was to deliver her baked maple barbeque chicken casserole at the elementary school's kitchen before driving back to the clinic for her morning appointments. Then she would return to the school for the community's annual noontime gathering.

Over her twenty-five years in Arlington, Vermont, Abby had come to think of the first Tuesday in March as her favorite holiday. Technically it wasn't a holiday – the Post Office was still open and mail was delivered, and the bank was open. All the businesses were open. At one time, the entire state stopped everything for Town Meeting. The citizens of Vermont's hamlets, villages, towns, and cities came together in their respective grange halls, schools, or municipal buildings for day-long business, reports, and votes at the floor meetings that followed the communal potluck feasts.

Abby was sad that Arlington – and most other Vermont municipalities – no longer followed the tradition of a day-long meeting, but she understood that modern work needs and travel took precedence nowadays, so she was glad the town was able to find a compromise of a half-day gathering that seemed to suit most of its citizens. It was important to Abby that a little bit of history was preserved in this oldest town in Vermont.

As she closed her front door and stepped off the porch to brace up the 'Save Our Arlington Rookery (SOAR)' lawn sign that had bowed under the snow, her cell phone rang. Her hands were too encased in a double layer of fleece gloves to answer, so Abby had to let the call go to voice mail.

When she was finally settled in the car as it warmed up, her bags and the casserole safely stowed in the back seat, she found a message from KT, the receptionist and LNA at the clinic.

'Hey, Abbs,' KT's bright voice sang out over the noise of the blowing heater. 'Just wanted to remind you that I'm stopping by Wanda's house to pick up her Holter monitor, so I might be a few minutes late. Be there as soon as I can. Bye!'

Katherine Townsend – KT, as she'd been known throughout town since she was in junior high school – was Abby's right-hand person. Her official title was 'Receptionist,' but KT was also the doctor's eyes and ears among their patients. In addition to performing the usual intake routine of patients' medical history and vitals, sometimes KT stayed overnight with or accompanied someone to medical appointments if friends or family members weren't available.

A licensed nursing assistant, KT also did occasional per diem work at the hospital fifteen miles south in Bennington. She always seemed cheerful, and her voice always carried a smile when she spoke. Abby knew how beloved she was with everyone in town, and she still couldn't believe her good fortune that KT worked with her. As busy as her right-hand person was, Abby couldn't believe she looked so much younger than her twenty-nine years of age. Not for the first time, she wished she had half the energy KT did.

As Abby drove to the school on the east side of town, she was heartened by the new placards that had sprouted up in snowy yards on both sides of Route 313 in the last two days. The usual campaign and political slogans and names were almost hidden by all the 'Protect the Rookery,' 'Save Our Herons,' and 'Speak Out for the WMA: Vote No' signs, many of them handwritten on big pieces of cardboard.

Looks like even the kids are getting involved, she said to herself as she gave a thumbs-up to a neighbor's youngster placing his own wooden sign next to his family's driveway. *Good on them,* she nodded.

She slowed down to the posted 25 miles per hour, passing the historic cemetery at the Episcopal Church where some members of the famed Green Mountain Boys were buried, and crept up to the intersection of Route 313 West and Route 7A behind a car of slower-moving tourists who seemed unsure how to navigate a major junction without a traffic light. She turned right onto Main Street, then made a quick left.

After a few hundred yards up the hill on East Main Street, Abby turned right into the parking area, waved to a group of women heading into the glassed-in school lobby, and parked. When she herself walked into the building, she was glad to see a bulletin board display of students' artwork that portrayed the heron rookery in the different seasons.

"That's one way to get around the ban on political signs at a polling place!" Abby called out to the teachers milling around in the office as she waved and made her way to the cafeteria down the hall.

Quick footsteps clacking on the linoleum tiles followed her. "Abby, wait up." Cindy Taylor, one of the two integrated arts teachers, had her arms full of manila folders that overflowed with paintings and drawings of more herons.

"Will these be useful today, do you think?" she asked when they stopped outside the cafeteria doors. "They're from all the different grades, and they've been working on these since January as they've studied the environmental implications in their science classes."

"These are remarkable, Cindy." Abby paused, thinking. "And yes, they're perfect. Let's put a folder on each table, so folks can look through them while they eat. More than one per table, if there are enough."

"That's a good idea. The kids will join us for lunch, so I hope people will ask them questions about their artwork."

Pushing through the double doors into the kitchen, Abby added, "And the science. Give the kids a chance to show off what they've learned."

"Excellent, Abby – I think there'll be a few excited young scientific artists," Cindy said with a smile. She shifted the folders so she could pull up a corner of the aluminum foil that covered the casserole dish Abby placed on one of the long prep tables in the kitchen. "Oh boy, that

5

looks good – one of my favorites. Thanks! See you shortly."

As Cindy left the cafeteria, she passed a young woman who seemed confused. She had the requisite casserole dish in one hand and a bulging cloth bag of condiments, bread, and cutlery in the other, and she was dressed in the preferred mode of 'Vermont casual,' but she was obviously unsure of what to do.

"May I help you? I'm Cindy Taylor."

"Is this where the town meeting takes place?" the young woman asked, looking past Cindy's shoulder into the now-open doors of the spacious lunchroom. "My name is Flora," she added a moment later, finally remembering to add her own introduction.

"Yes, right through there. You can take your dish into the kitchen. You're a little early, though. We won't start for a good four hours."

As if to agree with that, the bell on the wall above their heads rang once to alert the children who were in the hallways and still coming in through the front doors that they had five minutes before the 8:00 start of school. Cindy added, "Gotta scoot. Look for the long tables in the lunch room, Flora. You can put your stuff there for now."

***

Dr. Abby's last patient left the clinic by 11:15, and Abby and KT sat at their respective desks to finish up the morning's paperwork and notes. The quiet in the small office space was usual after a busy time of ringing phones and hustle and bustle, and both women welcomed the chance to catch their breath as they worked in the familiar and companionable silence.

Finally Abby put her pen down, pushed her chair back, and looked over to KT, who was in the process of shutting down her computer.

After KT called the answering service to let them know the office was now closed for the day, Abby stood up with a sigh, looked at her watch, and said, "Ready to leave the frying pan and jump into the fire?"

"Is it really going to be that bad, do you think?" KT had started to reach for her small, over-full backpack, but she secured the ever-present ballpoint pen in her thick strawberry blonde ponytail instead, her bemused expression hesitant. "If it is, I'm not sure I want to go. I can stay here and catch up on things …"

"Oh no, you don't," Abby said as she tried to turn KT toward the door. "You're going with me. You promised."

"I know, I know. And I will – you know I want to support you," KT said as she and Abby shrugged into their coats. "I just didn't think there was anything to worry about."

"I really didn't think there was either, until this morning. Cindy Taylor sent me a text a short while ago that she talked briefly with a woman who is new to her and who will be at the meeting."

"A tourist, maybe?"

"I kind of doubt it. Most tourists aren't interested in our politics, or they don't want to spend a whole afternoon with a roomful of strangers when they could be skiing or buying up the discounts in Manchester."

Abby turned from locking the front door and setting the security alarm. That was a new addition, one she didn't care for, but the clinic's insurance provider had deemed it necessary because of the few drugs on the premises. Making their way to the parking lot on the side of the small frame building, its narrow yellow clapboard slats indicative of their advanced age, Abby had to raise her voice over the noise of the town snow plow that drove by.

"It's probably nothing," she continued, "and I'm likely paranoid. The first thing I thought of, though, was that the developers had sent someone to eavesdrop."

As they settled into the old navy blue Forester and Abby backed out onto the road, KT declared, "At least this will make things a little more lively than usual."

Abby agreed and added, "So aren't you glad you're coming?"

KT's delightful giggle filled the car for a moment before she said, "Well, at least I know the food will be good!"

Town Meeting moderator Timothy Cahill took his time to stroll up to the microphoned podium, stopping here and there to talk with residents for a moment, to shake hands or share a laugh as he passed among the tables. Once at the podium, he picked up his bound copy of the town's Annual Report, waved it in the air, and called out

8

above the clean-up clatter and chatter in his official voice. "Get your reports out, everybody. We'll start in about ten minutes."

In the kitchen, Abby, KT, and Cindy consulted with one another over a series of print-outs as others worked around them, giving them space to spread out their papers on the long table. A tall man in a brown tweed jacket, blue jeans, and heavy hiking boots joined them.

Folding a dish towel that he proceeded to place on top of a small stack of casserole ware, his tone was encouraging as he asked, "Are you ready, ladies? It looks like you've got things well in order here."

"Thanks, Will," Abby said. "I think we're all set." She looked up. "What about you?"

Cindy Taylor added, "I'm glad the agenda has your kids and their essays just before us. That will be a good lead-in."

"Agreed," Will Putnam nodded. "And I can refer to the positive responses the children's art folders have received when I introduce the winners. Good job, everyone. This'll be a walk in the park."

"Let's hope so," Abby said, gathering up her papers. "That's the goal."

"Literally," KT added.

Cindy beckoned the three others a little closer and leaned in to whisper, "Before we go in, did anyone get a chance to talk with that new woman over lunch? Other than those folks coming in just now," she pointed through the kitchen porthole to two men and a woman, all three

9

dressed in black suits, who found seats in the back of the auditorium, "I haven't seen anyone else who might be from the developer."

"That's Spencer, et al," Abby growled, bending down to her papers again. "I'm surprised he's here. He usually sends his minions alone. If this vote does go his way, he should consider calling the project 'Spencer Minions Farm' rather than 'Spencer Meadows.' They've done all the work … seems only fair."

"Actually …" Will said, "that's not a bad idea, Abbs. Maybe I'll steal that when I'm talking with other folks. That's a good indication of the kind of neighbor he'd be."

"Or not," the others responded together.

Putnam continued, his voice low again. "Getting back to Cindy's question, I did get to spend some time with Flora. I don't think we have to worry there. She's new to town, on her own. She doesn't strike me as the type who could work with Matthew Spencer. She's much too quiet."

The three women looked at each other and then back to Will. "I don't know," Abby mused. "I can't help but think it's too coincidental."

"Well, we can't worry about it now," Cindy interjected. "Tim's got his gavel out, so we'd better get in there. We'll find out in due course."

The cohort of four fist-bumped together, and Abby declared, her Southern origins coming out, "Let's do this, y'all."

Once the meeting was called to order and the Pledge of Allegiance recited, the Town Clerk verified that a quorum was present. This was the point in the process where Abby always thought they should pay homage to, or at least acknowledge in some way, the presence of the framed print of Norman Rockwell's famous painting 'Freedom of Speech' that looked down on them from the wall at the back of the cafeteria.

When she had attended her first Town Meeting soon after her arrival in town, she was thrilled to learn that a few of the people there had been models for Rockwell as he worked on the painting that depicted a meeting day in Arlington in 1942. Even today she could see family resemblances among two or three of the townspeople who had, all those years ago, pointed out to her their grandmother or their brother or their neighbor. *Maybe I'll bring that up for next year,* she thought now.

The first half of today's agenda proceeded as usual. Last year's minutes and the yearly reports from the town's departments, boards, and groups were accepted with little, if any, discussion. Finally Tim Cahill announced a fifteen minute break. "Then we'll get to the part of the meeting we're all waiting for," he continued, "before we get to the elections."

As most of the people streamed out to the kitchen and the bathrooms, two of the three black-suited non-residents moved up to the front of the large room. They started to pull out sheaves of papers and file folders from their briefcases and spread them out on the long folding table to the right of the podium. Abby and her group did the same on the left side, none of them looking at or acknowledging the others.

At the same time, Will Putnam gathered seven teenagers into the front row of folding chairs and knelt down in front of the middle three. He talked in low tones as he went down a list written by hand on a yellow legal pad, like a coach with a team of athletes. The young women and men nodded, smiled, and encouraged one another with friendly shoves and nudges.

When Tim came to stand next to them, Will stood up and said, "Okay, everyone. When Mr. Cahill gives the go-ahead, I'll say a few words of introduction, and then turn it over to Heather, Jeff, and Melissa. Good luck, and remember to …"

"Slow down," all the teens supplied, "and *e-nun-ci-ate!*"

The sound of the moderator's gavel on the podium rang out and the roomful of excited conversation gradually quieted.

"Ladies and gentlemen," Tim announced as stragglers hurried to find seats, "we have a real treat before us now as the first of two special agenda items. Please welcome Dr. William Putnam, head of school at Putnam Academy, who will tell us more."

"Thank you, everyone," Will began after the small burst of applause died down. "The three young people you see here," he said as he gestured at the teens who now stood to his left, "are the winners of the Academy's first annual civics essay contest. The civics class – the rest of whom are here in the front row – wanted to participate in the 'Save Our Herons' campaign in some way, so we decided to explore how citizens of our towns, state and country can and do make a difference in movements to change the way we do things, sometimes even the way we practice our politics."

Will paused a moment to reach for a stack of light grey cards. "In the best tradition of Vermont's citizen representation," he continued, handing the cards to the other young people to distribute, "we are going to ask you to vote after you hear the winners' essays. Their names and the titles of their pieces are printed on the cards that are coming to you now. So," he said with the flourish of a proud parent, "allow me to introduce Ms. Heather O'Connor, who is a junior, Master Jeffery Bedell is a senior, and Ms. Melissa Reed is a sophomore."

Thirty minutes later, after the teens finished to applause and the meeting's votes on the essays were tallied, Dr. Putnam announced the winner.

"Congratulations to all our essayists, and the whole civics class, and especially to Melissa Reed, the winner of our first annual contest! I want to add that everyone who participated is a winner because they got involved in a matter that is vitally important to our town. I am very proud of all of them. Not only did they write and submit their words for us all to read and hear, but all seven of them have been working with the group you'll hear from shortly. And with that I'll turn the meeting back over to the moderator," Will finished, with a slight bow to Tim Cahill.

"Dr. Putnam? Before you finish …" Two rows back, Julie Thompson, Progressive state representative from Arlington, waved her hand.

"Please forgive the interruption, but I want to personally thank you and your students for your involvement on behalf of our town. I also want to commend these young people. No matter how things turn out," she continued, turning to involve the people around her, "I am confident that we've seen our future leaders here today, and I encourage your continued activism and critical thinking. Thank you – I look forward to working with you," she finished, applauding the students and the townsfolk around her.

Chapter Two

The Proposal

"Thank you, Julie!" Tim said as he returned to the podium. The woman in the black suit at the long table in front stood up, papers in hand. Apparently anxious to begin her presentation, she began to introduce herself, but Cahill touched her elbow to stop her for a moment.

"Ladies and gentlemen, and all voting residents of Arlington," he intoned, "we come now to the point of the meeting Dr. Putnam referred to. You all know that Matthew Spencer of Albany, New York, has applied to the town to develop 75 acres of the old Rushlow farm into what he calls 'Spencer Meadows Farm,' a combination high-end residential condominium complex and nine-hole golf course. The record will show that he has done so even though the Rushlow family has yet to sell the property or even put it on the market.

"You also know," Tim continued, "that this particular parcel lies just outside the rest of the Rushlows' land, which abuts the Wildlife Management Area of Lye Brook that Route 7 intersects on the east side of town. According to Mr. Spencer, the parcel is therefore eligible for eminent domain status. On the other hand, Lye Brook is federally- and state-protected as an IBA, an 'important birding area,' because of the heron rookery and other wildlife who call this sanctuary home. Any proposed development must go through rigorous screening to abide by the state's Act 250 zoning laws that were put into place to protect the environment. Mr. Spencer believes his proposed condo development is far enough away from Lye Brook that the Act 250 screening will find in his favor, and he has brought his representatives today to make that case.

"Many of our residents, however, believe otherwise. The Select Board feels this matter is too important for them to decide for the town, so – after several discussions, with and without Mr. Spencer – they voted to bring this before the Meeting for a public hearing and collective deliberation. Now we will hear from Ms. Sonia Aronson and Mr. Jacob Johnson of Spencer Associates, and then Dr. Abby Phillips, Ms. Cindy Taylor, and others from town will present their argument. There will be some time for responses afterwards," Tim concluded, "so please hold your questions and comments until then. And then we will vote."

He gestured and nodded to his right, and Sonia Aronson stood again. "Thank you, Tim," she said, looking not at him but at her colleague with a slight smile. Jacob Johnson rose and placed an easel with a large poster of an architect's rendering of the proposed complex in front of the podium.

While this was going on, Will leaned over to Abby and said, "Looks like Spencer's being true to form, sitting in the back while Sonia and Jacob do all the work."

When the associates finally looked up at the audience, they saw row after row of stony, expressionless faces and crossed arms. Even some of the older children, who had joined the meeting after school let out, followed suit.

Undaunted, Sonia's presentation started off eager and loud. "Matt Spencer is as much an advocate for the environment," she began, "as you all are in Vermont, as he made clear when he spoke at the December Select Board meeting last year. To put it mildly, he's surprised at the level of antagonism his proposal has received."

Her voice trailed off as her words elicited a round of shifting-in-chairs, and low grumbles and murmurs from the crowd.

"So that's why," Jacob interjected quickly, still setting up tripod-backed posters on the stage behind him, "we've prepared these graphics to show just how far away from Lye Brook such things as the effluent and drainage fields really will be. You'll see, too," he added, pointing to one of the posters, "that we've addressed Act 250 and town regulations about all the set-backs. I know some of you have been concerned about that issue."

The two associates alternated with each other, speaking and gesturing toward the graphs and drawings, for fifteen more minutes. As she started to gather up her papers, Sonia said, "We think that, once completed, Spencer Meadows will attract visitors, new residents, and additional monies to your town."

Sonia paused and looked at the people in front of her. "And who doesn't want more revenue for their town?" she asked with an attempt at a smile.

After a beat or two of silence and no response, Sonia finally closed. "All of this has been submitted to the Town Planning Board and is, I presume, available for public viewing." She looked to Tim Cahill for confirmation. Upon his nod, she and Jacob thanked the crowd and sat down.

In the ensuing silence, Abby, Cindy, KT, and the civics students from the Academy rose and moved among the rows of residents, handing one piece of paper, studded with bullet points, to each person. A gradual buzz spread through the room as more people read the list.

Abby waited a moment or two, letting the sound intensify as she stood in front of the podium. When she was sure everyone had a copy, she held up one of the pieces of children's artwork that had been on the tables at lunch.

"If the weather cooperates," she exclaimed, "we'll start seeing buckets and tap lines on the trees, and sugaring will start in a few days …" and had to stop at the small explosion of applause around her.

"Ellie Turner's picture," Abby continued, still holding the 11 x 13 painting aloft for all to see, "illustrates one reason so many of us are fighting for the rookery at Lye Brook. If Rushlow's farm is sold and developed, we'll lose one more place that is important to Vermont's way of life. Ellie is lucky because she knows, even at nine years old, how hard sugaring is, how demanding the process of making the liquid gold of maple syrup is, even with some of today's modern equipment. But, thanks to her grandparents, the Rushlows, she also knows the treasure of the old way – the big tanks on horse-drawn sledders, the fragrance of the evaporators' smoke billowing from the open slats on top of the sugar shacks."

She interrupted herself to add, "I know I'm not the only one who rolls all the windows down when I'm driving around and see that smoke, no matter how cold it is outside! There's nothing more exciting than that first sweet whiff, right?"

Abby let the townspeople enjoy the moment of anticipation. She took the opportunity to hand Ellie's bright picture – a snowy farm scene, a red barn in the background, and a pair of draft horses pulling a tank-laden skidder toward a brown-shingled shack with a slatted cupula in the middle of the roof – to the first person at one end of the front row. The picture made its way slowly up and down the several rows of people, and Abby continued.

"If we allow Spencer Meadows, or any development like it, we'll lose the sugarbush that Dan Rushlow worked and his children and grandchildren still harvest. Spencer Meadows isn't the kind of 'farm' we need," she insisted, crooking her index fingers in the air to simulate quotation marks. "What we need, what we want to *keep,* is Rushlow's farm."

Cindy Taylor, clapping along with the rest of the room, went to stand next to the architect's rendering that still stood on the stage. "We invite you to come up here and look at this image," she said. "When you get close enough to study it, you'll see that the half-mile driveway Spencer proposes to put in from Warm Brook Road cuts the existing sugarbush right in half. That's just the driveway. That doesn't begin to account for the damage that putting in that driveway will cause, all those 150-year-old sugar maples that will come down in the first sweep of the bulldozers or those that will fall later because their roots will be cut."

"There's nothing in this drawing, either," KT added, leaning against the front table, "to indicate the required greenbelt between the proposed development and the streams that flow from the Battenkill River and into the wetlands of Lye Brook. If the golf course, especially, is like most, the chemicals to maintain it will run off into the water table and the river with every rain. As Melissa said in her essay," KT reminded them, "the wetlands might be able to filter some of those chemicals for a while, but if the meadows that slope down to the river are turned over to condos, the waters won't stay clean for long."

"That's why we need to keep the greenbelt as it is," an old farmer called out from the middle of the room, unable to contain himself anymore. "And if that crap affects the water table, then the wells of all of us who live on Warm Brook will be, too!"

"As well as Lye Brook, the river, the wetlands, the herons and waterfowl, the beavers, and all the wildlife that relies on those waters," Abby agreed.

That single interruption quickly grew to the noise level of the pre-meeting communal lunch as others added their questions and comments.

"What does this mean for the Fisher Memorial Pines?"

"Think of how much this will add to the grand list and the town coffers when the condos are finished and people move in," a determined voice from the back of the room called out.

"No one's mentioned the increase in traffic, though," someone argued, "which will mean more wear and tear on the roads and more maintenance."

"That's right, and we might need to hire another constable …"

"We can barely afford to pay Charlie as it is, and he's only half-time," an old-timer chimed in. "Sorry, Cindy," he added to Charlie Taylor's wife, "but you know it's true."

"And you know the state troopers are cutting back, too," someone else added, "so we can't count on them to help."

"Will people in town be able to use the golf course, or is that for the condo owners only?"

"So is this fancy new place for all ages, or just for adults? If more children come into town, we'll need to hire more teachers. Just an hour ago, we saw how hard it is to pass the school budget now."

"Does Spencer expect the town to do the snowplowing of all those little roads in the winter?"

"What is this eminent domain business, and how does it affect Elnora?"

"How long will it take to build? I don't like the idea of construction traffic going in and out of town for a year or more."

"If Spencer's followed the Act 250 regs, I don't see the problem …"

And so it went for another several minutes. Finally the moderator held up his hand and asked the Town Manager and the Select Board to respond before the vote. Jayne Lester replied that most of the residents' questions had been addressed already in the Select Board meetings leading up to today's gathering and were in the minutes, which were printed in the Annual Report.

"Let me ask Mr. Spencer to address the eminent domain issue," Jayne said. "That seems to be a primary concern. Mr. Spencer, do you mind?"

From his seat along the back wall, Matthew thought to himself, *Shit! I sure as hell DO mind!* But he rose with what he hoped was a smile on his face and made his way to the podium. He kept his hands in his pants pockets as he walked so people couldn't see them shake.

"Mr. Spencer," Jayne said once he stood next to her, "perhaps you can start by explaining why you don't feel it necessary to approach Mrs. Rushlow directly with an offer and are using the claim of eminent domain instead?"

Spencer took the microphone the Town Manager handed to him and initially looked only at her as he talked. "If you look at the plot in person, you can easily see the land has fallen into disrepair and has no viable use."

He had to raise his voice as the crowd began to grumble. Taking a deep breath, Spencer turned to face them. "That land should be open to public use so people can enjoy more views of the wetlands, and eminent domain is the easiest and most direct way to make that possible."

An old farmer directly in front of Spencer said, "But your proposed development will block *Elnora's* view! And the only access to your condos goes right through her land – land that she keeps open so people can get to those views you're talking about."

"That land you want to take," a young woman a few rows back added, "is not in disrepair. It's a working sugarbush …"

"And has been for generations," another voice said, "as Dr. Abby reminded us a short while ago."

Spencer's associate, Jacob Johnson, seated again in the back, raised his hand to speak and stood up when Jayne Lester called on him.

"According to the information I've been able to find, the product from that sugarbush is not for sale, so the operation is a hobby, not a business. Therefore, we believe …"

"We believe," Spencer cut in, "that the people of Arlington will benefit more from the added tax revenues of new condos and updated recreational opportunities than from a hobby."

Jayne Lester nodded, thanked Spencer while indicating that he could return to his seat, and said, "Well, I think it's time to put this to a vote, Mr. Cahill, so I'll turn the meeting back over to you."

After a show of hands, it was clear that paper ballots were needed. Abby and her friends, joined now by Bud Belanger, who had arrived near the end of Abby's group's presentation, stood near the kitchen and looked at each other in surprise when the moderator called for the vote by ballot. The voting itself took only a few minutes, but the Town Clerk and a volunteer still had to tally the results.

Twenty minutes later, Tim Cahill moved to the podium and struck his gavel twice to call the increasingly noisy crowd back to order. "I don't quite believe this," he announced, shaking his head, "but we have a tie, right down the middle. The ballots were counted three times, and the result was the same each time. Sixty-three for the Spencer development proposal, sixty-three opposed."

The moderator waited a moment as a swell of voices grew louder than his own. As soon as they heard the gavel again, the townspeople quieted down.

"Move we table another vote," a gruff voice called out immediately, "to a special meeting on a date set by the Select Board, with the purpose of breaking the tie. We've been here too long already, and we still have to fill out election ballots!"

"Thank you, Roger. I was going to propose just that."

Several cries of 'Second!" rang out, and a resounding chorus of 'Aye!" followed Tim's call to adjourn the floor meeting. "Don't forget to hand in your ballots before you leave!" the moderator reminded the crowd, but his words were lost in the hubbub of moving chairs and conversations that erupted.

Matthew Spencer and his colleagues took the opportunity to slip out. He beat them to their cars by several steps.

"Well, that's hopeful," Sonia suggested when they stopped.

"Bullshit," Matthew snarled as he got into his black Escalade.

"At least it wasn't rejected out of hand," Jacob argued.

"This time," Matthew said. He put the car into gear and drove out, the tires kicking up a cold stream of messy slush behind them.

Chapter Three

Putnam Academy

A snowstorm barreled into southern Vermont the next day. Hurricane force winds screamed and howled from the west, whipping up snow drifts along all the major travel arteries and up against fences, stone walls, parked cars in driveways, parking lots, and buildings. Unlike most of the people in Arlington and the rest of the state, though, Alban 'Bud' Belanger, Jr., was in his glory. He loved days like this because it meant he wouldn't have to talk with anyone.

Bud wasn't anti-social. Far from it. He liked to be around others, he just didn't like to talk much. He preferred to listen and observe, especially after days like yesterday in the crowded meeting, and then gathering with the other heron advocates afterward. He needed a day of quiet.

Now Bud stood outside his two-room cabin, listening to the wind that sounded like a convoy of big rigs riding their air brakes as he watched the birds try to navigate the gusts among the myriad birdfeeders in his side yard.

Here on the edge of the Dorothy Canfield Fisher Memorial Pines preserve, the birds were somewhat protected from the worst of the winds. Every now and then the drifting snow got caught in spiraling updrafts that twisted and turned in all directions, pushing some of the

26

smaller birds in the air like the old copper beech and oak leaves that were blown out of the woods.

Sometimes it was hard to tell the birds from the leaves, but Bud knew the difference. He knew the winter drab of the goldfinches from the duller pine siskins, and he was glad to see that the male finches had started their slow morph into the cheerful yellow plumage that was most familiar to people.

Most people couldn't see the little brown creepers, even when they scooted themselves like tiny vortices up and around the pine trees and oaks on which they were so perfectly camouflaged, but Bud could. One of his favorite sights was to watch the nuthatches ratchet headfirst down the trees at the same time one or two brown creepers went up. He knew the white-breasted nuthatches were bigger, more talkative, and cheekier than their shy cousins, the red-breasted nuthatches, likening them to upside down mini-penguins. When he talked to them, he called them his 'little zippers.'

Just as a pair of cardinals flew in, the scarlet male to one of the handmade cedar chalet feeders and the sunset-colored female to the snowy ground underneath, an ATV-mounted snowplow pulled hard into Bud's drive and scattered all the birds.

Dammit, Bud muttered to himself. *So much for the quiet.*

The young driver waved Bud over as the engine sputtered to a stop.

"Morning, Bud! Beautiful day, isn't it?"

"That it is, Teddy. That it is. What can I do for you?"

"The engine doesn't sound right. There's so much snow to clear off the walks, I don't want it cutting out on me before school starts. I'd appreciate it if you can look at it for me."

Bud had hoped for a few more minutes with his birds before starting work, but he took his job as maintenance supervisor at Putnam Academy seriously and he knew the students had to get to their classes soon. He and Teddy, a young man from town who did on-call seasonal work around the campus, were soon draped in snow as together they explored, diagnosed, and finally fixed what turned out to be a clogged exhaust line.

Teddy's friendly wave as he drove off seemed to signal the birds that all was safe again, and Bud spent a few more minutes in their company as they flocked back to the feeders. Eventually he looked at his watch, went back inside, had one more cup of strong black coffee, and got ready to walk over to the school.

He considered himself lucky to live where he did, to have the job that he did. Now thirty-eight years old, Bud had worked at the Academy for almost twenty years. He had started part-time with the landscaping crew. Eighteen months later he was offered a full-time position in maintenance, an increase in salary, and the choice between an on-campus two bedroom apartment and the small cabin on the outskirts of the property.

By then, no one was surprised that Bud chose the cabin. He loved the campus's old, formal, brick and wood buildings, and he enjoyed working among the teachers, staff, and lively teenagers, but he needed to be as close to the woods as possible.

The Putnam Academy, a private high school that funneled into the Ivy League and 'little Ivies' like Dartmouth, lay on the northwest side of town. In something of a 25-acre triangle between the north-south Routes 7 and 7A and Route 313 west into New York State, the school had been founded by family members of one of Vermont's first governors. One of its most popular courses was still political science, and some of its students went on to graduate studies at the School of International Training across the state in Brattleboro, a step in a career of diplomacy.

Most of the Academy's population of fifty were boarding students who lived in two of the original family's buildings that had been added to and modernized as needed over the decades. A few day students from Arlington and nearby towns swelled the ranks. According to the founding charter, five merit scholarships were awarded each year to qualifying Vermont pupils, regardless of financial status. Only members of the scholarships committee knew who received the awards.

In addition to the strenuous academic and community service standards, the high school required the young people to participate, as they were able, in arts and music classes, athletics such as track and field, lacrosse, basketball and baseball, downhill and cross-country skiing, even snowboarding, and horsemanship and dressage.

William T. Putnam, DLitt, now Head of School and Professor Emeritus, was the last of the direct descendants of the founding family. He lived on the more affluent west side of town near the campus in what was generally accepted as the local 'gentleman farmer's manse in the Shires.'

A former Republican legislator in the state House of Representatives, Will was drawn bit by bit into Abby's environmental concerns by her active commitment. Eventually he ran for the state Senate as a Democrat in the mid-1990s and won two terms. While in office, he sat on committees that studied and proposed geothermal heating, solar, and wind energy options, and he sponsored and co-sponsored anti-development bills. After he left the Vermont senate, he wrote a book about his environmental switch, copies of which were in the stacks of the Academy's and town's library and bookstore.

Semi-retired at 58 years of age, Will taught the year-long civics class and occasional short-term courses, some with Bud on Abenaki culture and customs. In fact, the two had an appointment later in the morning to finalize plans for the vernal equinox sweat lodge and ceremony in two weeks. Will always credited Bud for giving him the final push into the progressive environmental agenda.

The two men had known each other for years. In a true 'opposites attract' relationship, Will's extroverted personality and Bud's quiet, gentle manner complemented the other, and they became fast friends soon after Will re-joined Academy life when he retired from public service. He enjoyed watching Bud live and model his Native American heritage without actually teaching it and, as he himself had done, how the students emulated him.

When Bud showed up at Will's open office door at 10:30 AM, Will greeted him with a hearty handshake and an enthusiastic hug. "It was good to see you yesterday at Town Meeting."

"Good to see you, too. Abby and her team had a good presentation, eh? And your kids did a bang-up job." Brushing snow from and removing his dark purple buffalo plaid barn jacket and matching hat, Bud apologized for bringing the snowstorm into the office.

"It's hard not to on days like this," Will responded. He turned to look through the wide three-over-three sash window behind his desk. "You and the crew are doing a great job keeping things clear, as always."

"Thanks. Not many students about, though. I know this is one of those days when the kids wish we were on the same closing roster as the town and county schools."

Will agreed as he sat across from Bud, already seated in one of the captain's chairs at the broad oak pedestal table. "That's something I'm going to bring up to the Board at our next meeting. Again," he emphasized. "I want to look into remote video feeds for situations like this. We have the technology and know-how. I just don't know if our Internet dead zones can be circumvented – which may be something Abby and her committee can address, given the mountains and the dearth of cell phone towers around here. At least for now the teachers have the option to postpone or cancel their classes, and no students are penalized for staying in or staying home."

"Speaking of canceling," Bud added, "any word from Abby about tonight's meeting?"

Will shook his head. "As far as I know we're still on, but that may depend on Gina and if she keeps the diner open. It's early yet – if I don't hear by two or three o'clock, I'll give Abby a call and let you know."

"The snow's already letting up a bit," Bud said, looking up toward the windows. "This looks like it may turn into more of a sugar snow than anything. The roads and walking should be much better by the afternoon."

"That's good news. What do you say we go get some lunch before the kids hit the cafeteria, and we'll have room to look at your plans for the equinox sweat?"

Bud and Will said little as they walked through the almost-empty administration building and two flights down to the cafeteria in the basement, as though they felt the need to mimic the silence. Once in the dining hall, though, the noises and activity coming from the kitchen seemed to stimulate them, and, pushing their trays along the food line, they joked and laughed with the cooks and servers.

As they reached the desserts near the end of the line, Will noticed a new server behind the counter. "Well, hello there," he greeted Flora. "I saw you at the meeting yesterday, didn't I? You picked quite a day to start a new job."

She looked at him for a moment, her head slightly tilted as she tried to place him. "You do look familiar," she responded, "but I saw so many people yesterday …"

"Of course! Forgive me. I'm Will Putnam. And this," he continued, turning to his left, "is Bud Belanger."

Flora and Bud nodded to each other and smiled.

"That's right, you did the part with the civics essays," she remembered. "They were impressive – the students *and* the essays."

"Thank you. I'll pass that on to the kids. I thought so, too." Will noticed that others were coming into the dining room and nudged Bud. "Well, we need to get to work. It was nice to meet you and welcome to the Academy."

"Thank you. Nice to meet you, too."

When they were settled at a table near the back of the room, Will leaned over to Bud and said in a near-whisper, "Yesterday Abby thought that young woman might be a 'plant' from Spencer, but I guess this proves otherwise."

"Maybe." From the vantage point of his back against the wall, Bud could see Flora without appearing to stare. "She seems friendly enough. Kind of shy, but there's nothing wrong with that. Did you catch her name?"

"Damn, no, I didn't. Her nametag said 'Flora,' though. Cindy said that's the only name she gave when they met before the meeting."

Will buttered a yeast roll to dip into the steaming homemade Swedish meatballs and added, "But we'll find out more in due course, I'm sure. First we have to plan this sweat ceremony you insist we have the week before Easter, so dig in and let's get started."

Their easy laughter rose above the hall's increasing noise level and caught Flora's attention. She looked up from placing more desserts into the food line's cooler and studied the two men for a moment. Finally she focused on the student now standing before her.

"What can I get for you? The lemon meringue pie is really good today."

Chapter Four

Capital Diner

Abby Phillips and Cindy Taylor were the first to arrive at the diner, driving together in Abby's navy blue Subaru Forester. Before they could get out of the car, another Subaru, a metallic royal blue Impreza coupe, pulled in next to them and KT hopped out. She opened Cindy's door for her before she bent into the back seat of the Impreza to gather up a fallen-over pile of ten or twelve emerald green file folders.

"Here you go," KT told Cindy with a laugh as she plopped the folders into Cindy's waiting arms. "All present and accounted for."

"Oh good, thank you. I was afraid some parents took them home yesterday."

"A few almost did," Abby said as she, too, came to stand between the two cars, "but KT noticed just in time and went around to rescue the purloined artwork."

Now holding open the door to the diner, Cindy nodded. "I've long said that KT needs to be on the rescue squad."

"For more reasons than one," Abby said, patting the younger woman on her parka-clad shoulder. She pretended to whisper to Cindy, "Last I knew, that cute EMT is still on the squad, isn't he?"

KT's long strawberry-blonde ponytail bounced a little as she shook her head at the good-natured ribbing. She was used to her friends trying to set her up with dates, and her clear green eyes sparkled in response. "Yes, Matt's still there. Thing is, he's even busier than I am ..."

"Who can possibly be busier than you?" a voice exclaimed as they reached the middle of the glassed-in back room. As she spoke, Gina Frost, owner and manager of the diner, distributed napkin-wrapped cutlery on a large round table that was covered with a crazy quilt-patterned oilcloth.

"With all the patients' errands that you do, you're essentially full-time at Abby's clinic." Straightening up, she added, "And you're on call at the hospital, and you house-sit and pet-sit in what you call your spare time. I don't know how you have time to breathe!"

"At least we know she eats once in a while," Abby noted with a smile, "when we make her come to our meetings here."

"And I do eat breakfast here every Tuesday," KT added.

"That you do!" Gina agreed.

By now the four women had been joined by Bud, Will, and three of Will's civics students, and there was a bustle of greetings, removing coats, and finding places around the table. A few other town residents straggled in, waved and spoke to the group, and sat at the nearby tables Gina had pulled closer so the other townsfolk could participate in the meeting if they chose.

Known to locals as 'Gina's Place,' the Capital Diner was located on the far north end of Main Street – which was designated as 'Historic Route 7A,' 'Old Route 7,' or the 'Ethan Allen Highway' on maps and road signs – and was named to reflect Arlington's claim that the town was the first capital of the state of Vermont.

Built in the mid-1950s, the diner had been in Gina's family – distant relatives of the iconic poet Robert Frost – since 1963, and they had added updates and more seating over the years while still retaining the features of the original diner atmosphere.

A long counter with attached stools was in between the front door and the busy now-modern kitchen, and a section of booths and small tables opened up to the large room where the meeting was taking place. Through the glass, patrons could see the new deck and pergola that had been built for summer dining over the Battenkill River. Any available wall space held prints, photographs, and old newspaper accounts of such famous former residents or nearby neighbors as Dorothy Canfield Fisher, Grandma Moses, Norman Rockwell, and, of course, Robert Frost. The glassed-in room was sometimes used by local artists for shows and sales, and some of their works were always hanging on the walls or metal joints, or displayed on lightweight shelves.

The menu was full of traditional homemade diner fare, and Gina made sure to feature two or three meals a day that had become local favorites over the years. Every regular customer had his or her own coffee mug, which they retrieved themselves upon arrival or found waiting – and full – at their usual seats. Gina's Place had become the primary distributor for the local sugar makers, and a big sign out front boasted that *only* Vermont maple syrup was served. An old hand-hewn bookcase next to the cash register held five shelves of the golden and amber goodness in bottles, cans, molded candy, and other products.

As soon as everyone was seated and had placed their respective orders – and three servings of the best onion rings in southern Vermont to share among them – Will cleared his throat.

"Well, friends, it looks like we've got more work to do. I expected some of the usual curmudgeons might vote in Spencer's favor, but I can't believe there was actually a tie."

"That was a surprise," Cindy agreed, shaking her head, "and a big disappointment."

One of the students asked, "When will a final decision be made? What more needs to be done?"

Everyone now looked to Abby, halting personal and side conversations. "We've got a couple of months, I think, but it depends on how much attention the Select Board gives each side. Spencer wants to start digging as soon as he's permitted to bring in heavy equipment, so that's mid-to-late May at the earliest."

She paused and nodded her thanks as the server placed a plate of chicken parmesan in front of her. After Will and KT, on either side of her, were served, Abby continued. "One thing I want to do tonight is form a small group to do some last-minute research on environmental regulations, both state and federal. There might be something we've missed that could stop Spencer in his tracks."

"I nominate Will for that group," Bud said immediately. Others nodded and someone said, "Makes perfect sense, with his legislative experience."

Abby looked at Will with the question, and his affirmative "Of course" was applauded with claps, hands slapping the table, and stomping feet.

"Okay," she continued, "let's eat before everything gets cold, but everyone think about how you can help. We need more members for the research group – Will can't do it by himself, after all. I'm going to call Sherman Weeks to see if he'd be willing to do a little *pro bono* work for us. And before we leave tonight, I'd like to finalize an early agenda."

Abby stopped and looked around at the people gathered at the tables. "I think we also need an official representative to the Select Board, someone who can go to their meetings and report back and forth between them and us."

Over the sounds of cutlery against plates and bowls, another student suggested, "What about someone to meet with the Spencer folks, too?"

"Are you volunteering, Jeff?" Abby asked with a smile and raised eyebrows. "For either or both, I hope?"

He thought for a long moment and finally said, "Actually, yes. If you think I can help, I'll do both, as much as I can around my schoolwork," the tall blond senior finished. He looked toward Will for permission.

"I think that's a wonderful idea," Dr. Putnam affirmed. "We can probably even arrange a little academic credit. It is civics, after all."

"Hell yeah!" Cindy's spontaneous response drew enthusiastic laughter from around the table.

Abby's wide smile was as much for the efforts of all those around her as it was for the young man. She leaned over and said to KT, "I just love this town."

Chapter Five

Decisions, Decisions

It all started with a drive in the summer before her final year from the medical school at the University of Vermont. A few spontaneous hours turned into a quest.

Abby Phillips spent as many of her weekends as possible traveling around the state. She wanted to get a broader sense of its people and places than she could get in Burlington, the relative metropolis on Lake Champlain up in the northwest corner of the state. She knew she wanted to stay in Vermont, but Chittenden County was too busy for her. She wanted to practice medicine where she was needed, and there were already plenty of doctors so close to UVM.

Using a fold-up map and her trusty DeLorme *Gazetter*, Abby designed what she came to think of as a labyrinth and, weather permitting, set off early every Saturday morning to a different part of the state. It didn't take her long to realize this was going to be a difficult decision-making process – there wasn't a region or population that she didn't fall in love with.

She drove alongside vast acres of spruce and balsam trees in the quiet semi-alpine landscape of the Northeast Kingdom and spied several moose next to the almost-empty roadways. The wide open skies and nighttime starfields, the family of red foxes jumping in gleeful abandon in a summer meadow above Lake Willoughby, the gentle rain over Lake Memphramagog, the sweet fragrance of the air and the wildflowers …

Abby remembered almost every minute of that first weekend. The moments she held most dear were her secret momentary lapse as a scofflaw when she unintentionally drove left into Canada on a side street in Canaan instead of right, and the afternoon she finally saw a pair of loons at a friend's lakeside cottage in Wolcott. The thrill that went through her when she heard their primeval calls echo among the tall mountains and across the dark glacial waters would stay with her forever. She understood well why the locals called the Kingdom 'God's Country.'

When she followed the autumnal tapestries of her labyrinth southward, Abby soon found that glimpses and patches and panoramas of God's Country were found in all the other parts of the state as well.

The north-south corridor that bordered the Connecticut River between Vermont and New Hampshire, anchored by the quirky 'hippie' town of Brattleboro in the southeast, was another piece of heaven.

A little northwestward, Woodstock's reputation for wealth and the arts was well-deserved, she discovered, but its people were as unpretentious as she could wish. The White Cottage roadside eatery later became almost a pilgrimage destination on her occasional summer drives up to White River Junction's VA hospital. And no trip there was complete without a visit to Quechee Gorge, the 'Grand Canyon of the East.'

Her journeys along what the weather forecasters called the spine of the Greens took her deep into the Green Mountain National Forest and the little towns, villages, and hamlets of central Vermont nestled within its embrace. There weren't the wide open vistas of the Kingdom in this part of the state, but almost every curve in the road revealed a view on which to feast the eyes.

Towns and cities here bustled with activities of all kinds, in all seasons, but there were always hidden back roads to explore and to quiet the heart. Abby never tired of the covered bridges, rushing streams, cool tunnels of deep shade over dirt roads. She loved it when she chanced upon lighted gazebos on town commons that were dressed up for winter, springtime fields exuberant with the first cheerful dandelions, summer agricultural fairs, autumn's craft fairs under sparkling skies and the jeweled colors and hues of the foliage.

After nearly a year of traveling around the state, Abby narrowed her regional choices to Addison County and Bennington County, both on the western side of the state. She was sorely torn between the two.

The farmland in so many parts of Addison County that folded down to the shores of Lake Champlain, that exciting first glimpse of the lake when driving north out of Middlebury on Route 7, the harvested fields that welcomed migrating waterfowl by the thousands at Dead Creek Wildlife Management Area, the lake itself and the Adirondacks behind it ... The Champlain Valley called to her, but, if she traveled just a few miles north, it quickly became too crowded for her.

The southwestern county of Bennington reminded her most of home. Abby had grown up near Asheville in the mountains of North Carolina, and the small towns from Dorset down to Pownal on the Massachusetts border were similar to many of the mountain towns she had known all her life, especially when she got off the main roads. When she discovered Arlington, between Manchester and Bennington, she felt like she was home again.

She was surrounded by history and possibilities. The townspeople were proud of their connections to the arts and education. Abby found out that Norman Rockwell had lived in Arlington for a while back in the 20th century and had hired a few locals as models for some of his famous paintings. If she drove south on Route 7A to Shaftsbury, she could easily see the still-maintained stone summer cottage that Robert Frost sometimes used as a retreat.

During her first lunch at the Capital Diner, she learned that Grandma Moses had been a frequent visitor to town from nearby Salem and Cambridge, New York, about 20 minutes west in today's automobiles. And one of the ubiquitous tourist brochures noted that Dorothy Canfield Fisher, founder of the Montessori schools, lived and wrote here – which meant that Abby had to visit the town library named after Fisher, as well as the Preserve. When she later discovered the Academy and the Preserve bordered each other, Abby thought the juxtaposition was perfect.

Most important, there appeared to be no local medical practices. Bennington's hospital was almost 25 miles south, Rutland's medical campus was an hour north, and all of Albany's hospitals were a little more than an hour away. There was room for her here, easy access to places and events to explore in four states – Massachusetts was less than half an hour south, and Connecticut was only an hour's drive – and a general atmosphere that encouraged both roots and strong branches among its varied populace.

Even though she was 'from away,' townsfolk soon realized she wasn't a flatlander. The Smoky Mountains had raised and nurtured her, so Abby knew how to fit in quickly. She did two things right away: she registered to vote and she got a library card. She volunteered or helped out whenever and however she could. She became involved in church and community groups and activities, always going early to set up or staying late to help clean up. And she drove a Subaru, the unofficial vehicle of Vermont.

Twenty-five years later, Abby, now 55 years old, still believed that Arlington reflected the best hospitality of the South in which she was raised and the strong independence of the North Country. She had left her beloved Smokies because the mountainsides were becoming too developed. Too many communities there showed no sign of stopping new roads up and down the ancient wooded slopes, adding more and more lighted homes among the few trees that were left. Most Vermonters, on the other hand, were determined that their ridgelines and mountains would remain green and free from the scars that new building left behind.

Now, as she drove the familiar back way into town after a visit to a patient at Southwest Vermont Medical Center in Bennington, she looked at the dashboard clock and made a last-minute decision. She had a couple of hours before her next patient at the clinic, so instead of making the left turn onto Route 313/West Main Street, she kept straight on Main Street.

The gradually rising temperatures of the four days after the snowstorm were perfect for the start of the sugaring season, and Abby's car windows were open a little. She knew it was still a little early to expect the sweet fogs from the evaporators, but somehow 40 degrees always felt warmer in late winter than it did in the fall. Abby inhaled deeply of the fresh air as she turned up the neater a notch. She was on a mission: her annual pilgrimage to the tropics.

Usually she went to Equinox Valley Nurseries sometime during February, when she couldn't take the ice and cold anymore, but this year's snow depths and record-setting low temperatures had kept her close to home. The one or two days that had been nice enough to venture north to Manchester had been occupied with patients or meetings, so she needed this last-minute and delayed retreat.

She always looked forward to spending time with the resident cockatoos and brightly-colored macaws and responding to their squawked greetings. The heat and humidity of the winterized greenhouse, and the oxygenated air from the plants, made her feel like she'd had a rejuvenating spa treatment. Today was even windless and warm enough to buy a plant or two without subjecting it to frigid temperatures between building and car and then car and her house.

Once she was on her way again, refreshed after her reunion with the birds and the plants, Abby drove back south on Route 7A to her house and clinic. This stretch of road took her through some of her favorite old farmlands of the Shires. The traffic was sparse for such a nice day, and she took her time.

She could see the Battenkill was starting to flow faster now, swelling with the first of the sun-warmed snowmelt. In a few weeks red-wing blackbirds would fill the reeds and bushes along its banks, but Abby looked for them anyway, just in case. The afternoon sun and shadows were almost right.

She knew, too, the turkey vultures – or buzzards, as she called them – would return first, when the temperatures created warm updrafts upon which they would soar in search of roadkill and small animals emerging from their winter hibernation. Privately Abby always tried to be the first among her friends to spot the earliest arrivals. When she drew alongside the polo fields that were shared among the shire towns and schools, she pulled over onto the wide shoulder, parked and turned off the engine, and scanned the blue sky through her front windshield.

A few minutes later, with no sightings, Abby started up her Subaru and put it into gear. Just as she pulled back onto the road, a black Cadillac Escalade passed her going north at fifteen miles or so above the posted speed limit of 45 MPH. If she hadn't known that Matthew Spencer always drove too fast for the winding roadway, she could easily identify the big five-door vehicle as his from the tinted windows and the orange New York vanity plates that proclaimed 'SPENCE' for all the world to see.

Must be taking his fancy lawyers up to Manchester, she muttered to herself. *I wonder what's going on?*

"You should've followed him!" KT declared when Abby returned to the clinic with a few minutes to spare before her next appointment and told her about Spencer's unexpected appearance.

"I did think about it," Abby laughed, "but I knew I had to get back here."

She handed KT a fully-blooming Easter cactus to adorn the reception desk and turned to remove a potted jade plant from its insulating wrapper. The jade would go in the west window of her study in the back of the house, to get the afternoon light that she so loved.

"Have you heard from Jeff Bettell about last night's Select Board meeting?" Abby asked, reaching for the patient chart KT handed to her. "I know he planned to start his new 'assignment' there, before he sets up something with Spencer."

KT shook her head. "Nothing yet, but he should have something soon. He's probably still in class."

Abby nodded absentmindedly as she leafed through the chart. "Okay, let me know if he calls," she said, waving over her shoulder as she walked down the hall to Exam Room 2 and back to work.

Abby would soon find out that Matthew Spencer had been on his way not to Manchester, but to the little town of Dorset on its northwestern border. His two associates were with him, as were two potential investors. When Abby saw them, they had just come from viewing the Rushlow farm property and would spend that evening in the refined elegance of a local bed and breakfast establishment.

If she had paid closer attention, Abby would have been alarmed that Spencer's usually-immaculate Escalade was much more snow-encrusted and dirt-splattered than the road conditions should have generated. When she found out later that Spencer had gone off-road and into the sugarbush to show the property to his investors, she was furious. But the phone calls about that were still to come.

Chapter Six

An Uproar or Two

Soon after Spencer, et al, had settled into their rooms and were now gathering again downstairs, Matthew realized he had made a mistake with his choice of lodging. Not for himself, so much – though he did prefer more spacious accommodations than this historic Colonial afforded, however graceful – but for his young clients.

Before he'd even reached the ground floor, Matt could hear Janice Thompson, wife of Eric, asked the teenaged daughter of the owners who tended the desk where she could buy some snow boots.

"I know I can't walk around here in these things!" she giggled, lifting up one stiletto-heeled foot to show the teen. "You're just the right age to know the good places!"

"Well, the feed store should still have some in stock," Linda offered, "or if they don't, you can try the hardware store across the street."

"The feed store or the hardware …?"

Matthew hurried over before Janice's confusion got the better of her. He lightly took hold of his client's hand as he explained slowly to the teenager, "I doubt that she wants those rubber boot things."

"Of course not!" Janice exclaimed. "Those are for barns, aren't they?" She took a breath and looked at

Spencer with growing concern. "We're not going to look at barns tomorrow, are we, Mattie?"

"No, Jan, we're not. Don't worry."

Trying now to placate both his client and Linda, still patient behind the desk, Matthew continued to try to help. "I think you're probably looking for leather boots, right? With the low heels, like you wear at home?" *Which you should've brought with you,* he added to himself. *She knew there was snow up here, and that we'd have to be out walking. Why the hell couldn't she have ...?*

But he breathed in, slowing his inner tirade, and said as if thinking to himself, "There are bound to be other shops around here."

"Everything here in town is closed," Linda said, "but," she added quickly, seeing Janice's frown, "most of the outlet shops up in Manchester should still be open for a while."

"Outlets?" Janice squealed. She grabbed hold of her husband's elbow and looked at Spencer. "How far away is Manchester? Let's go now!"

Linda's answer of "About fifteen minutes" was almost lost on Janice as she ran as fast up the stairs as she could in the tall, narrow heels. "I'll just get my coat!"

A moment or two later, Linda held open the front door as they all filed out, Sonia and Jacob tagging along and asking about dinner. Handing several advertising brochures to Eric, who was last in line, Linda smiled and said, "These might help. You have a good evening now."

The morning room of the B & B was quiet and filled with early sunlight when Matthew entered and joined his associates at one of the five small Queen Anne-style dining tables. Sonia and Jacob had already started their breakfasts, and Jacob greeted his boss with a raised glass of orange juice. Sonia looked up and nodded, to which Matt responded with one of his own, but none of them said a word.

The quiet continued as he pulled out his Smart Phone, sat down, and proceeded to check his messages. Spencer scrolled down to find an email that had come in the previous night.

"Son of a bitch!" he muttered as he read, and again as he put the phone down on the table hard enough to rattle the cutlery a little.

"What's going on?" Sonia asked, now checking her own phone, just in case.

As if he hadn't heard her, Matthew picked up the single-page embossed menu and glanced through the listed fare. Sonia was used to this, so she continued to consult her phone while she waited.

Finally, after giving his order to the server, Matt leaned forward, elbows on the table, and whispered, "Some asshole reported us to the Arlington constable and the Town Manager. Said we tore up part of a sugarbush when we were at the Spencer Farm property yesterday."

"What the hell is a sugarbush?" Jacob asked.

"How the hell do I know?" Spencer said through gritted teeth. "All I saw was snow and mud and more snow."

"And no road," Sonia added. Then as an afterthought to herself, she said softly, "You heard what a sugarbush is at the Town Meeting."

"And therein lies the problem," Matt said, sitting back in his chair, referring to Sonia's first comment. "According to the citation, no motor vehicles are allowed on such terrain until the middle of May."

"That's absurd!" Sonia blurted, and Jacob added, "How does anyone know we were there? I didn't see anyone."

Spencer shook his head. "Neither did I. The only thing I can think of is ..." He took a moment to think. "Remember we passed that old pickup parked on the side of the road before we drove up the hill? There must've been someone inside who saw us. And now the whole world knows – what a bunch of busybodies and gossips."

He fell silent as the server placed his breakfast before him and Eric and Janice came in. Eric could tell something was going on, so he let his wife chatter on about her shopping spree while they ordered their food. As soon as the server disappeared into the kitchen, he looked at Spencer.

"Did we interrupt something? We can go to another table ..." Eric suggested.

"No need," Matt said, keeping his voice down. "We just got word about something I need to look into before we head back, so I'll have to stop in at the town office before we go to the property again."

To look at Matthew Spencer, one wouldn't think him an angry person at first. Uptight, perhaps. Controlled, yes. Right now he was both uptight and trying to control the anger that friends and colleagues felt always roiled just under the surface, but he was trying to keep his 'client face' more visible.

Tall and lean at 6 feet 3 inches, his pale brown hair was cut as close to the scalp as possible without leaving it bald. Below his high forehead, his narrow grey eyes pierced through the slim lenses of the stylish glasses he wore all the time. Growing up, Matthew's glasses had been much thicker, the refraction seeming to make his myopic eyes appear crossed at times, especially when he looked intensely at someone.

Spencer was glad that age and technology had gradually corrected that effect, but his eyes were just as penetrating as he loomed now over the town manager's desk in the small paneled room, and his strident tone carried into the public office on the other side of the thick wooden door.

Jayne Lester sat at attention and watched the display, her hands folded loosely on the desk, as she let Spencer rant for a while. When he finally needed to take a breath, Jayne said into the moment of quiet, "You were cited because you abused the ordinance, Mr. Spencer. It's as simple as that.

"No," she stated, holding up a hand when he started to speak again, "let me finish. That ordinance is one that most, if not all, towns in Vermont have in place to protect the sometimes fragile dirt roads and fields. They are wet and soggy from spring melt right now, and will continue to be until after mud season. Once the roads dry up and potential damage is minimized, usually around the middle of May, we can allow traffic again. So you will just need to wait.

"I know it's hard to understand," she finished, standing up and moving to the side of the desk, "for people who aren't from here, but the citation stands and you are responsible for the fine."

"I don't give a flying … *FLIP* … about the fine!" Matthew almost shouted, stopping his favorite expletive just in time with the internal reminder that he was not in his own office. "I need access to the property for my trucks a lot sooner than May!"

As if acknowledging his attempt at verbal constraint, Jayne Lester touched Matt's elbow to guide him gently toward the door. Looking up at him from her height of five feet and four inches, she stood at the now-open door.

"There might not be a need for equipment of any kind. Even with access, though, Mr. Spencer, heavy equipment and construction trucks are even more restricted. Especially so close to protected land. Besides," she finished, ushering him into the larger office, "it's much too early for all that. May I remind you that you are not the owner of the property – yet – so you're lucky you weren't cited for trespassing as well."

Jayne Lester opened the building's front door as she added, "But you are welcome to *walk* there any time you like. Like the farmer did whose sugarbush you tore up. Thank you for coming in, Mr. Spencer."

As soon as she closed the door behind him, Jayne turned around and caught Abby Phillips' eye. She had seen Abby come in as she ushered Spencer out of her office. Abby clapped her still-gloved hands, and they grinned at each other.

Jayne took a deep breath. "That special meeting can't come soon enough, as far as I'm concerned. I want this to be over."

"But, my goodness, what a few phone calls can do in the meantime," Abby said, taking off her gloves, her brown eyes still twinkling. "Is that true, by the way?"

"Is what true?"

"That heavy equipment has to wait longer to use those roads?"

Jayne shrugged her shoulders and put a finger to her lips. "I really don't know for sure," she mused. "If it isn't, it should be."

"Damn skippy!"

Chapter Seven

Developing News

At Gina's Place the next day, Elnora Rushlow sat in a back booth facing the door of the diner. When Abby walked in and looked around, Elnora waved her over. Gina came out of the kitchen at the same time, carrying something in her hand, and together they joined their friend as they slipped into the banquette seat opposite her.

As soon as she'd removed her jacket, Abby reached across the table. "Elnora, I'm so sorry about the damage Spencer caused the other day. He had no right to be there, and he knows it."

"It's a good thing Billy was there, though," Elnora said, "and that he reported it to Charlie. I heard you were in Jayne's office yesterday when Spencer went in to complain."

"I was, and she was magnificent," Abby chortled.

Gina shook her head slightly. "You know it won't stop him, though. I'm glad you asked us to meet, Abbs. Maybe we can come up with something to …"

Abby placed her left arm around Gina's shoulder as she interrupted. "KT sent me something last night I want to run by you all," she said, leaning back in the booth, "but I'll wait until the others get here. So," she continued, pointing to the 8 x 12 handwritten posterboard 'Help Wanted' sign Gina had placed on the table, "why are you looking for more help?"

"Mary, Brad, and the girls have to move down to Pownal next month," Gina explained. "I hate to lose my best worker, but her folks need help with the farm. She's already lined up jobs at the Blue Benn and the Sunny Side in Bennington."

"That won't leave much time to help her folks," Elnora said. "Will Brad stay at Mack Moulding?"

Gina nodded. "It's not that far a drive, and nothing for those two old Vermonters. They figure this way the girls can finish out the school year here. Brad will drop them off in the mornings and Mary will come up to get them in the afternoon between shifts. So we may get to see them still, at least for a while."

"And we can go visit them, and help at the farm if needed, too. Which reminds me," Abby said, looking at her watch, "I wish the guys would get here."

As Gina stood and took up her sign, she said, "Well, let me find a place for this, then we can start our lunch, anyway. They can catch up."

She turned as the diner's door opened and closed, and saw that Mary was already with the customer. A moment later, at a front window, Gina called back to the others, "Bud just drove up. I'll get the menus and be right back."

On his way to the back booth, Bud waved to Gina, Mary, and the kitchen crew. He stopped briefly at the table where Mary had seated the previous customer and then joined the others. Elnora moved closer to the wall and patted the seat, silently inviting him to sit beside her.

"Sorry I'm late. I had to help some kids reattach the smoke stack's collar on the evaporator."

"No worries," Gina said, sitting next to Abby again and handing around the menus. "We're still waiting on Will." Her smile of greeting grew wider as she asked, "So sugaring has started, then?"

"In earnest," Bud concurred, as did Elnora. "The temperatures this week have been perfect."

"Well, I know a few folks who won't be in for a while, then. Elnora," Gina added, "I can fix up some suppers for your crew, 'cause I know they'll be hungry. I'll get those going as soon as we're through here. Bud, maybe you can pick them up this afternoon and take them over?"

"Be glad to."

"Thank you so much, Regina," Elnora said with a quiet smile that also included Bud. Elnora was the only person in town who called Gina by her full name now, a habit left over from her days of teaching at the elementary school when Gina was a student. "I know they'll appreciate that."

"I'm off tomorrow, too, so I can make up a week's worth and take them over. That'll get 'em through the hardest part anyway." Gina leaned forward to ask Bud in a whisper, "Who is that young lady you spoke to when you came in? I feel like I've seen her before."

Bud and the others leaned in to keep the conversation close. "You probably saw her at Town Meeting," he explained. "She works at the Academy, just moved from Bennington less than a month ago. All I know is her first name is Flora."

"Ah, and here is Will," Elnora said, looking up at the door's tinkling bell.

"Finally!" Abby said, turning around.

Like Bud, Will stopped at Flora's table and spoke with her for a moment, and then he made his way to the back booth. Pulling up a chair to sit at the end of the table, he too apologized all around.

As the others' food arrived, Will gave the menu back to Mary and said, "Just coffee, please, when you get a chance. I'm late because of a lunch meeting I couldn't get out of. It was boring as hell, but at least they fed us pretty well."

Abby wasted no time. "Hopefully this meeting will be better," she responded. "Elnora and Gina already know about Spencer's run-in with Jayne Lester yesterday. Have you two heard about it?" she asked Bud and Will.

At their mutual nods, Abby continued. "Oh good. First, then, I really appreciate y'all coming at such short notice. KT sent me something last night that sparked an idea I'd like to talk over with you, and I couldn't wait.

"This is a print-out from Cornell," she continued, passing around a paper, "about a course they now offer at the university. KT found it on Facebook and thought we'd be interested. As you see, it's called 'Civic Ecology.' I expect most people have heard about 'sustainable agriculture' and 'regenerative gardening.' This looks like it goes those one better, because it gets whole communities involved, rather than the usual image of a lone gardener or farmer."

By now Will was holding the piece of paper. "This is what some of the kids in our civics class referred to in their essays," he interjected.

"Exactly! I thought you'd be interested in this, Will." Abby pushed aside her plate as she got more animated. "I thought some of them might like to check out the Website for more information. For one thing, I'd like to get them – and the whole town – even more involved in our campaign to stop Spencer's development of Elnora's farm."

Everyone at the table gave Abby their full attention, putting down their utensils or coffee cups as they waited for her to continue.

"Thanks to you all and others, we already have a good little coalition going to protect the farm, the herons, and the wilderness area, and we've done good work. But before the next vote, I'd like to expand both the group and our work. I think we should form a cooperative of farmers and supporters to *buy* Rushlow's farm, if Elnora's willing. We can all work it, we can ..."

"We can form a CSA!" Gina jumped in.

Elnora looked confused. "What's a CSA?"

"That's community-supported agriculture," Gina explained. "More and more towns and cities, and some farms, have programs that make local produce and products available to customers who subscribe to buy pre-sized amounts. You can arrange to get bushels, baskets, or boxes on a weekly, monthly, or seasonal basis. You have to go pick them up, but each CSA puts the containers together – in other words, they do the 'shopping' for you by harvesting and packing up the produce – so it's all ready when you get there."

Gina stopped to draw in a breath and Abby leapt back in. "And that's just one possibility. You can sell your milk in more places, Elnora, or rent your goats to clear brush … but whether a CSA emerges or not, the point is we're all trying to save your farm and the nearby land in our small way. I think it's time to commit to something bigger, on behalf of the town, the environment, you and your family, and all of us."

Elnora shook her head slowly, her forehead creased in worry. "It sounds like an awful lot of work, even more than we already have to do. I just don't know if I'm up to that."

Bud took her hand gently. "If I see where Abby's going with this," he said, "you won't have to do anything you can't or don't want to do. We'll do it for you, or arrange for it to be done. That's the beauty of a co-op. Everyone is invested – literally, because we buy shares – and everyone contributes in various ways according to their abilities."

"I like that," Will said, as if musing to himself. "We'd be making an *investment* that can only benefit everyone …"

"Except Matthew Spencer," Abby reminded them, and she looked in turn at each of her friends around the table. "It will take some doing, I know, and we'll need legal and fundraising help, but I think we can do this."

"I agree," Gina declared. "I'm in."

Will and Bud nodded in agreement. Elnora hesitated, looking down at the table, while the others waited in patient silence. Finally she lifted her head. "Me, too. But you'll all have to help me understand how this will work."

"We'll find out together, honey," Abby said, taking the widow's small hand. "We'll find out together."

Gina slapped her hands down on the table and stood up.

"We're going to buy the farm!" she sang out and then announced to Mary, "This calls for a celebration. Free dessert for everyone!"

Chapter Eight

Good People

Bud stayed behind after the others left. He had heard Will say a cheery 'See you tomorrow!' to Flora on his way out, so Bud stopped at her table. She had just finished the last bite of her surprise dessert of lemon meringue pie.

"May I join you?" he asked with some trepidation. "I don't want to intrude ..."

"You're not intruding at all," Flora assured him. Her shy smile and silent hand gesture toward the opposite seat invited him to sit.

"Thank you. May I buy you a cup of coffee? I don't want to keep you if you've got other plans, but I'm waiting for some things from the kitchen and thought I'd take the opportunity to welcome you to town a little better than over the lunch counter at school."

He rose a little from his seat, held out his hand, and said formally, "I'm Bud Belanger, Maintenance Supervisor at the Academy."

Flora took his hand. "Thank you, Bud. It's very nice to meet you. I'm Flora MacDonald." She took a moment to collect and stack her dirty dishes and place them at the end of the table. "I'd love a cup of tea to top off this good food."

Bud asked Mary, as she passed them, for Flora's tea and a cup of coffee for him. "It is good food," he nodded, "the best in town for years."

"How long have you lived here?" Flora asked.

"Almost thirty years. I was born in the Northeast Kingdom, where my family is from, but we moved down here after my dad was injured in a logging accident so his sister could help with his care."

"You never wanted to go back? The Kingdom is rightly named – it's so beautiful."

"It is," Bud agreed. "But back then jobs were hard to find, and we were so isolated from medical and other resources, it was easier downstate, especially for a family with young children." He smiled his thanks to Mary when she brought their beverages, his coffee in the large brown pottery mug that had his name on it.

"I do miss the wilderness," he acknowledged quietly, and Flora could almost see the sigh in his deep-set black eyes, "but I'm very lucky that I'm still in the woods here, and I do go back occasionally. There's still the family camp to tend to."

As if she knew another subject would be better, Flora pointed to the cups now before them. "Your own personal coffee mug. Nice!"

Mary, picking up the used dishes, said with a smile, "All our regulars have their own mugs. If you're here long enough, you'll have your own, too."

Bud looked up after adding some sugar to his coffee. "I'm sorry to hear you'll be leaving soon, Mary.

It's a good thing you're doing, though. I know your folks will appreciate the help."

"Yeah, I really hate to do this to Gina – and of course I'll miss everyone terribly – but it's time to join the sandwich generation, like so many others have had to do. And," Mary added, her hand on Bud's shoulder, "Pownal's just down the road, so I expect we'll run into each other."

"Well," Bud said, "now we'll all have a reason to do more in Bennington than just our food shopping. I'll be sure to stop in to the Blue Benn for coffee whenever I go down."

"You better had," Mary declared, patting his shoulder before turning to take Flora's dishes into the kitchen.

"She will be missed," Bud said as he watched her. Turning his attention back to Flora, he said, "On a happier note, I hope, I'm impressed that you were at Town Meeting a couple of weeks ago. Had you even started work yet?"

Flora shook her head. "No, I started a couple of days later. I'm not a native, but I've been in Vermont long enough that Town Meeting has become very important to me. And I thought it would be a good way to meet people … or at least start recognizing people when I see them about town."

"Are you all settled in? Is there anything I, or my friends and I, can help with?"

She shook her head again. "Thank you, I appreciate the offer," she replied, then added softly, almost as an embarrassed afterthought, "but it doesn't take long to move into a trailer."

Bud responded in kind. "No, that's true. But if you find you need anything, please don't hesitate to ask. We're good people here, and we help each other whenever we can."

"I've noticed that already," Flora said with vigor. "I think I'm going to like Arlington."

"We hope so," Gina said, a bright twinkle in her brown eyes. She had come up to stand at the end of the table, her arms full of large foil baking pans that she had filled with her homemade shepherd's pie, garlic breadsticks, salad greens, and various pastries and cookies. "Pardon me for interrupting, but these are ready, Bud, whenever you are."

"Then I'd better get them over to Elnora's right away. I just hope I can get it all there without stealing a few samples," he teased, standing up and putting on his coat. As he reached for his gloves, he managed to retrieve Flora's order ticket without her seeing.

"And I need to get back to work. It's almost suppertime, and I know the kids will be hungry," Flora said, checking her watch. "What a nice afternoon off," she added, standing as well and holding her jacket. "Thank you so much for the dessert," she said to Gina. "Bud, thank you for the good conversation and the tea. I'll see you in the dining room again, I guess."

Gina looked between Flora and Bud two or three times. "Wait," she ventured, "forgive me for prying, but do you work in the cafeteria at the Academy?"

"In food services, yes. Just part-time, though. For now at least. That's all they had available when I applied."

"Well, well, well. Don't put your coat on just yet," Gina said with a broad grin. "If you have time, I have a little bug I'd like to put in your ear …"

Now standing at the cash register and counting out his and Flora's tips, Bud turned long enough to say, affection in his voice, "Flora, I'd like you to meet Gina Frost. Gina, this is Flora MacDonald. Somehow I think you're going to become fast friends."

***

Abby and Cindy Taylor huddled close together in the one momentarily sunny corner of Elnora's back deck. Typical for late March weather, the afternoon had turned cold after almost three days of moderate temperatures, the blustery wind bringing squalls of snow and rain. Situated as they were in the valley between Glastenbury Mountain to the northeast and the Taconics to the west, Arlingtonites knew how to take such quick changes.

As they watched the latest squall line obscure the sun with its sooty clouds, Cindy warned Abby she might have an influx of young patients soon. "I swear half the kids in school were in shorts yesterday – some were even in sandals – and it barely made 45 degrees!"

Abby nodded knowingly. "Yep, rushing the season is the perfect prescription for colds and flu. Happens every year at this time. But I do so understand the urge," she added, pulling her knitted wool scarf closer around her neck as a blast of cold and snow swirled around them.

Cindy shivered and headed back to the door that led to the elongated interior of the 1850s white clapboard farmhouse. "I've got to go in. You coming?"

"In a minute. I just want to look around a little."

Cold as she was, Abby turned into the wind to look westward for a moment. The front of the house, and this part of the deck, faced that way, and she could see the tops of the Taconic Range foothills beneath the clouds. Tall and graceful white paper birch trees, lighted into gold by an unexpected shaft of sunshine, were grouped into three separate stands in the front yard. Though it wasn't obvious because of the piled-up snow, Abby knew the middle – and oldest – group was actually a nine-trunk clump of its own, and Elnora's treasure. On the other side of the yard, next to the driveway, an ancient sycamore, massive and speckled, balanced the delicacy of the birches.

Across the road, a stream trickled with snowmelt in a rocky, terraced ditch and would soon flood into the Battenkill for a few days. A bit of a slope lay behind the stream, topped by an old stone wall. Birches, smaller sycamores, copper beech, sugar and red maples, white and red pines, hemlocks, and a few scraggly spruces grew in what used to be old farm fields that leveled out among the waist-high brush that would be wildflowers in the summer.

Beneath the snow in front lay an expanse of almost an acre that would, in five or six more weeks, turn emerald green and canary yellow with spring's new grass and dandelions. Abby smiled to herself at the thought. It was a long time coming, she thought, but the wait was always worth it. One of the things she most admired about

Vermonters was that they never mowed down the first dandelions, so starved for color were they by that time.

She remembered one time she'd visited Elnora and Dan Rushlow that had been a case of being in the right place at the right time. They were seated on the back deck on a perfect late-May afternoon. As they talked, Abby noticed quick movements out of the corner of her eye. Looking to her right, she saw goldfinches by the dozens swoop down to the ground in noisy, chirping waves.

The Rushlows and Abby suspended their conversation and watched as the birds, grass, and fluffy seedheads became as one, the colors mingling and merging so it was almost impossible to tell which was which. A short thirty minutes later, the goldfinches flew off as a group, and all that remained were the waxy, bent, and empty dandelion stems.

Dan Rushlow had smiled at Abby, nodded his head and said, "*Now* we can mow the grass."

She had never seen such a sight before, and she hadn't in the several years since. Now she sighed, both at the delightful memory of the occasion itself and from missing Dan.

As she turned to go back inside, she said to herself, *This is for you, Dan. And Elnora. And the herons.*

Chapter Nine

The Squire of the Shires

Will stood at the wide bay window in the center of his second-floor office, looking out at the fine snow coming straight down. *It's the first day of spring, damn it,* he thought to himself, shaking his head. *Poor Bud,* he added almost aloud as he watched his friend trudge across the common in the center of the five buildings of the Academy campus. *Even he's getting tired of this long, long winter.*

That was in part, Will knew, because the weather had wreaked havoc on Bud's careful plans for the students' last week on campus before the short Easter break. He was supposed to have started the sweat lodge today for the equinox ceremony on Friday, four days from now. Before that Bud had promised he would help the science students finish boiling the sap they'd collected from the sugarbush and bottle the syrup, but the temperatures had gotten too low again for the sap to flow.

Will remembered Elnora's dismay yesterday at the meeting at her house. 'The kids had just that one day of boiling last week,' she'd said, 'and that was rushing it a little.'

And here was more snow. It wasn't even a proper sugar snow – the slow, fat, heavy flakes that presaged warmer days and seemed to hang in the air as if someone were holding up a veil of white among the trees – and colder air was due to come in overnight. No wonder Bud was trudging.

I wish Bud could live in my house, Will thought. *Then he could be a little closer, at least.*

Over a century ago, when Arlington had been the state capital, the elegant buildings on each side of what had become the campus common had been the homes of Will's ancestors. Then-Governor Thomas Putnam and his family lived in the large house that now served as the administration building. Will's office was in what had been the sitting room of the master suite, and a few volumes of the governor's personal library still lived in the floor-to-ceiling bookshelves on one side of the room. The former servants' quarters on the third floor had been turned into offices for the deans and teachers. Administrative and business office staff were on the first floor, along with an overflow classroom or two and the reception area. The basement held the kitchen, dining hall, and the mail room and student mailboxes.

The largest of the other three Federal-style buildings were directly across from this one and now housed all the boarding students. The former homes on either side had been modified over the years with some Colonial influences. Now the still-gracious structures held classrooms, a couple of large art studios, and the science and computer labs. A small but up-to-date library, connected by the Internet, when it worked, to the Canfield Memorial Library in the middle of town, took up the first floor of the old home on the eastern, right-hand side of the compound. Official gatherings and school ceremonies took place in a spacious and bright reading room in an annex that had been added in the middle of the 20th century.

Because the campus fronted the town's recreational fields – through the snow Will could just see the scoreboard above one of the baseball diamonds – the school shared physical education facilities and resources with the town. Three maintenance sheds were in a row off to the western side of the rec area, one for landscaping equipment and tools, a smaller one for seasonal storage, and one for recycling and composting.

Will's residence was almost hidden from sight. Off to the side and near the top of the drive that led to the dormitory, the former carriage house for the resident ancestral Putnams was on the edge of the woods, its brickwork almost covered now in English ivy.

He didn't often reflect on his privileged ancestry anymore, but as Will continued to stare out the window, his thoughts turned to the various politicians and lawmakers, churchmen and churchwomen – all of whom had been expected to be active members of the Episcopal Church in town – and policymakers in his lineage and wished he had a fraction of their know-how for the new plan Abby had in mind.

Thank goodness for Sherman Weeks, Esquire, who was stomping up the snow-covered walkway at that moment. Will was surprised to see him at yesterday's gathering. Palm Sunday was always a full day at church, and Will knew the 76-year-old almost always took a nap on Sunday afternoons. He also knew the widower had a bit of a crush on the Widow Rushlow and even more of one on Dr. Abby, so maybe that's why the attorney was there.

Whatever his intention had been, Sherman had added some much-needed discernment to the fast-paced conversations that filled Elnora's living room yesterday, and Will was glad they had the chance to talk more today.

In addition to their lifelong friendship, Sherman had been something of a champion for Will every time he'd even thought of bucking tradition.

Will was the only one in the long line of his family who was not confirmed at St. James' at the age of twelve or thirteen, waiting instead until he came back to the church in his late twenties. He was the only one, too, who had left the Republican party. That was bad enough, but Will's mother, Cora, had been sure his defection had been the cause of his father's heart attack. That he had still been in state office when he did so, and then to declare as a Progressive, sent her into paroxysms of apoplexy even now.

Sherman Weeks had stood behind Will at each juncture, to support and encourage him when others couldn't or wouldn't. As Senior Warden Emeritus, Sherman was there when they buried William T. Putnam, Junior in the ancient churchyard, but Will knew his presence was more than one 'old-time' cradle Episcopalian marking the passing of another of his generation. If Sherman had not been one of the officiants, Will would have insisted that he sit beside him and next to his mother as one of the family.

Will shook his head of the swirling thoughts and memories when he heard energetic clomping on the wide center-hall staircase, and he turned to greet his old friend as he knocked on the jamb of the open door.

"There he is, folks – the Squire of the Shires!" Sherman teased, coming into the room. He knew Will didn't like that nickname because he'd spent over two decades trying to downplay his unofficial position in the town's society, but he had no doubt Will would take it with the familiar affection he intended.

Will's quick grin proved him right. "The Squire and the Esquire meet again," Will said, adding his verbal imprimatur to the joke and shaking Sherman's hand in a strong grip. "Long time no see!"

"One of the true joys of living in a small town," the attorney acknowledged with a smile, sitting on the blue and gold damask-covered settee across from Will's desk. Will sat in a matching armchair to Sherman's left and watched him pull out a yellow legal pad from his canvas portfolio.

"Goodness, you've done a lot of work already," Will said, seeing the pages of notes on Sherman's pad fan out onto the gleaming top of the Queen Anne coffee table between them. "And thank you for doing this *pro bono*, Sherm. We really appreciate it."

Weeks nodded in response and retrieved more papers from his still-bulging bag. "I wanted to get started on the forms for the non-profit and 501-C-3 right away. It's going to take a while to get everything filled out."

"Did you all decide on a name for our new enterprise after I left yesterday?"

"Not yet, but they've narrowed it down to four possibilities, so we're a little closer. We'll need to decide soon, though, so I can file with the Secretary of State and beat, or at least meet, Spencer's timeline."

Will leaned forward and clasped his hands together. "I just can't wrap my head around why he thinks he's got this in the bag," he mused. "Do you think the man is delusional, Sherm? I mean, seriously," he continued as

75

Weeks chuckled. "Yes, he mentioned an amount to Elnora months ago, but he hasn't made anything close to an official proposal – at least not to her – nor has he produced any earnest money."

"And yet he acts as if his claim of eminent domain will carry the day and the property is already his," the attorney agreed. "Or should be."

"Do you know anyone on his legal team?"

Sherman shook his head. "No, but I will need to find out who he's working with so I can notify them right away. I'm glad we've already established the Board of Directors. That will speed things up a bit. By the way," he added, looking up from the papers on the table, "I'm quite impressed with that young student of yours."

"Jeff Bedell?"

"Yes. He's going to go far."

"I'm pleased you think so. I do, too, and I'll be sure to pass on your words to him. That will mean the world to him."

Will stood as he asked Sherman, "How 'bout I go get us some lunch and we can keep working in here? I have something I want to talk with you about, and we won't need to battle the noise of the cafeteria."

Matthew Spencer's ears should have been ringing, had he not been talking with his associates via the Blue Tooth in his left ear. The three of them were trying to line up two or three more couples who had expressed interest in the investment possibilities of Spencer Meadows, and

Matthew was on his way back to his office on Corporate Woods Boulevard on the outskirts of Albany.

He was not in a good mood. His mother had called from Florida and wanted him to look for some mail she needed to finish her and his father's taxes, so he'd had to leave the office and drive to Center Brunswick and the house in which he'd grown up and still lived in as caretaker for his snowbird parents.

Sonia had called while he was still there, and her news didn't help his mood. None of the couples wanted to make the trip from New Jersey to Vermont during the upcoming Easter weekend. Try as he might – even to calling each couple himself – they could not be convinced.

As was his wont, Spencer took their refusal as a personal affront. Even with Sonia's and Jacob's assurance that the couples were not backing out – that they wanted to go to church at home, not in a strange congregation in another state – Matthew couldn't stop the feeling that he'd been rejected.

It didn't help that Sonia informed him, as he was backing out of the driveway in Center Brunswick, that Will Putnam from Arlington and someone named Sherman Weeks had called and wanted to speak with him as soon as possible.

"Who the hell are they?" Spencer yelled into the Blue Tooth and the empty space of the Cadillac as he pulled onto NYS Route 7 toward Albany. Sonia reminded him they were from Arlington and added the news that Weeks was an attorney.

"Fine, fine. I'll return the call when I get back to the office," Spencer promised with a heavy sigh. Navigating the potholes, heavy traffic, and frequent stoplights through Troy was getting on his nerves more than usual today. He took another deep breath, trying to be more patient. It wasn't Sonia's fault, after all. She couldn't help it that Easter was important for some people.

"So I'd like for you and Jacob to go over the investors' list again," he said as he finally merged onto I-787, "and see if you can find some people who don't go to church on Easter. Please," he added, remembering in time to be polite. For a moment anyway.

"I'm going to Vermont this weekend and someone – anyone – has to go with me."

Chapter Ten

Transitions

A stray shaft of early morning sunlight, pale though it was, found its way around the back of the house and into Abby's study, instantly brightening the butter yellow walls around her. As if they'd choreographed it beforehand, both Abby and her little all-black cat, on a pillow beside her on the couch, stretched at the same time into the unexpected warmth.

Not for the first time, Abby thought back to the day when Gilda had chosen her from all the other visitors at the rescue shelter. She had jumped up into Abby's lap as soon as Abby sat down, started purring right away, and settled down for a long nap. Abby had already decided to adopt the year-old cat, but when a similar momentary burst of sun came through the skylights of the cat room and gilded the diminutive cat's black fur into a field of glistening diamonds, she knew she'd made the right decision. She only hoped the cat, whom she immediately named Gilda, had as well, but she knew cats well enough to trust that feline instinct.

Now, almost fourteen years – and a few white streaks – later, she stroked Gilda's short, thick fur, still so soft it almost couldn't be felt. The cat's tiny front paws curled around Abby's fingers, and Abby complied with some gentle belly rubs. The computer and emails could wait.

After their brief interlude, Gilda decided she'd had enough affection for a while and flounced off, following the sunshine to the kitchen and the rest of her breakfast, and Abby pulled the computer back onto her lap. A new email had come in from Bud in the interim.

'Hi Abby – Apologies for intruding so early on your day off, but this'll be quick. Just wanted to let you know that Will and I have decided to postpone tonight's sweat lodge because of the weather. If it were just snow, that'd be OK, but the wind is supposed to be wicked as the front comes through. We don't think it'd be a good idea for the kids to go from the heat and steam into such cold, and we don't want anyone to go home sick for break.

'Thanks for volunteering to be on hand tonight, but now you can have a whole day and night off! We're going to reschedule for next month – if we can't observe the vernal equinox, maybe we can do something for Earth Day. Thanks again!'

Abby's response was short but heartfelt. She was disappointed for Bud and the students because she knew how much they were looking forward to the ceremony, but she was glad for the extra time for herself. Now she could take her time with her plans to make the brief 25-30-mile trip over into New York State and what she called 'Grandma Moses country.'

The close proximity of the iconic painter's Salem and Cambridge landscapes was one of the reasons she'd chosen to live and practice in Arlington. She took advantage of it whenever she could, almost always returning with a new print or memento to add to her collection.

Now that she had more time today, Abby put the laptop aside again and patted the cushion beside her to invite Gilda back up on her return. Together they settled more deeply into the couch for a short cat nap. Just before she closed her eyes, Abby saw an empty space on the wall over the desk that could hold another photograph or small print, and she breathed a contented sigh as she drifted off to sleep.

Today was also Flora MacDonald's first full day at her new job at Gina's Place. She'd spent a few hours with Gina and Mary late last week to learn the routine, observing and shadowing Mary as she served the customers. Today she would wait on people and Mary would shadow her.

Flora had already served the early morning regulars and was re-filling their personal mugs with fresh coffee when KT came in and sat in a booth for two near the counter. Mary took down the only iced tea glass on the mug shelf, made KT's iced coffee in the glass etched with butterflies, stirring in milk and three sugars, and handed it to Flora as she picked up a menu.

"KT doesn't need a menu, hon," Mary said. "She always has the same thing. I've already put in the order, but why don't you introduce yourself when you go over? I think you two will like each other."

Flora stepped over a customer's black Labrador who was sprawled on the floor between the counter and the dining room and placed KT's glass on her table with a shy, friendly smile. "Hi, I'm Flora. Mary said you always get the same thing, but I can take your order if you'd like something different."

KT smiled in return and shook her head, her lush ponytail bouncing as usual. "Hi, Flora. I'm KT. That's the letters K and T, not Katie," she added. "Nice to meet you, and welcome! Mary's right – if it's my day off, it must be eggs benedict day."

"It'll be ready soon, then. Can I get you anything else?"

"No, thanks. I'm good." As she unrolled her silverware and put the napkin in her lap, KT asked, "Is this your first day here? I don't remember seeing you last Tuesday."

Flora nodded. "It is. I'll be here three days a week until the end of the school year, and then full-time after that."

"Excellent. This is a great place, and you'll meet some wonderful people."

"And more than a few characters," Mary added as she came up and put KT's breakfast before her with a flourish. "And it is excellent, indeed. Flora's going to take my place when I have to leave. Until then," she continued, putting a hand lightly on Flora's shoulder, "she's going to be a busy gal, working here and still in food services at the Academy, too."

KT's eyebrows rose in appreciation. "Wow. Impressive. I bet you don't cook much at home, then, being around all that food."

"You're right about that – at least not as much as I should."

"That's pretty obvious," Mary said with a loud but mock wistful sigh. "She's such a tiny little thing for being so tall."

Their laughter greeted an old farmer in a brown wool barn coat, green-checked flannel shirt, khaki-colored overalls, and muddy rubber boots who came in the door just then. A slight, but not unpleasant, aroma of manure followed him in.

"That's what I like to hear in the morning," he called out for all to hear, "beautiful women laughing!" He put down the Yorkshire terrier he carried in his arms, who scampered over to the wagging black Lab for a mutual sniff, and joined the now-full counter of regulars to a cheerful chorus of 'Hiya's and 'Mornin''s.

Mary nudged Flora with her elbow. "And here's one of those characters now," she said fondly. "Come meet Mr. Billy."

As they both went back to work, KT waved to Flora and Flora said with a smile, "I'll bring you some more iced coffee shortly. Enjoy your breakfast."

***

Matthew Spencer was in a slightly better mood by Wednesday afternoon. His associates had managed to convince the husband of one of the couples in New Jersey to make the trip to Vermont over the holiday weekend, and

Spencer had just made reservations at the Pillars Inn for their rooms and dinner on Saturday night.

He picked up the phone and called Jacob in the outer office. "We're all set," Spencer confirmed when he picked up. "You sure you can't come? I checked just in case, and there are still a couple of rooms available."

Jacob tried to hide his sigh, which was easier to do over the phone than if Spencer had made the effort to open the door and come to his desk in person. "Matt, I told you my ex-wife wants me here so the girls can have what she calls a proper Easter. And I want to be here," he emphasized. "This is the first holiday since we broke up, so I ..."

"Well," Spencer interrupted, "check with Sonia again, then. Maybe she's changed her mind."

"She doesn't have a choice. She's going to visit her dad in Schenectady. They made plans a long time ago, to accommodate her brother's travel schedule."

Spencer leaned an elbow on the glass-topped desk and made no effort to withhold his muttered growl as he rubbed his forehead in his palm. "I know, I know."

Jacob waited while Matthew was quiet on the other end. After a moment or two, Spencer said, "Listen, let me talk with her and ..."

"She left about twenty minutes ago, to pick up her brother at the airport, and she won't be back until tomorrow morning, But she did leave me a note," Jacob added, talking over Spencer's groan, "that you need to be sure to call the people in Arlington before close of business. They've been calling every day."

"Shit! Why won't they leave me alone?" Spencer turned his chair to look out the first floor window, as if the view of the parking lot would help. "All right," he sighed. "I'll call now, get it over with, I guess." And he hung up.

The next morning, Will walked across the almost-empty campus toward the administration building. In an hour or two there would be a flurry of activity as the boarding students left for Easter break, but for now things were still and quiet. Only the almost-tentative birdsong kept him company, as if the cardinals – thanks to Bud's tutelage, he was proud to say he knew just which bird was singing – weren't sure if the heavy snow flurries would let them announce spring just yet.

He welcomed the silence as he thought about his phone conversation with Matthew Spencer yesterday. He dreaded telling Abby, Sherman, and the others that Spencer was coming up again on Saturday, but as soon as he got up to his office, he stopped at his assistant's desk to let her know he'd be on the phone for a while.

Pamela Guillemette commented on his dour expression, so unlike his usual morning cheerfulness. "Uh oh … You look like you've had bad news, Will. Anything I can do to help?"

"Thanks, Pam, it's just Spencer again. I've had to schedule a meeting with him and one of his investors for Saturday afternoon. The timing isn't great – I'd hoped for some writing time this weekend, but Spencer insists on hijacking the holiday, so it looks like the Co-op group needs to have a strategy session before that. Thanks for the offer, though," he said, taking off his coat as he walked. "I'll let you know after I call a few folks."

She got up from her desk and followed Will to the threshold of his office. "I'll hold all non-essential calls," she said, her hand on the doorknob, "until you say otherwise."

"You're a gem, Pamela," he answered as she pulled the door closed.

Almost forty-five minutes later, Will emerged again. He sat down in the old captain's chair in front of Pam's desk, his long legs stretched out before him, ankles crossed.

"Well," he reported, "that was fun."

"So what's going on?" Pam asked. She had automatically assumed what Will called her 'patient teacher' position and expression when she leaned back in her chair as if prepared to listen to the concerns of yet another student.

Will made no secret of the fact, to her or to others, that he considered Pam the unofficial Dean of Students. As long as she stayed at the Academy, he promised himself once more, there would be no official person or position with that title because there was no need.

"There are a whole lot of unhappy people," Will said. "No!" he added quickly, jumping out of the chair and pacing back and forth in the wide alcove at the top of the stairs that was Pam's office. "To be honest, they're pissed and I don't blame …"

Pam threw up a hand to stop Will's pacing. "At least slow down a little," she said, her eyes twinkling with the mutual understanding of their long friendship, "so you don't fall down the stairs. Take a deep breath and then start from the beginning."

He stopped and looked at Pam with a rueful grin. "Yes, ma'am. You're right. As always."

Will took his deep breath, sat back down, and continued.

"The thing I'm most angry about is Spencer's apparent expectation that we'll all just fall in line behind him and rearrange our schedules to fit his. When I talked with him yesterday, he could not grasp the concept that folks have plans for this weekend. It's a holy time for a lot of people, but that doesn't seem to matter to him."

Will could feel himself getting worked up again, so he took another breath. "At least I was able to insist that I meet with him *before* supper on Saturday, not afterwards like he wanted, so I can still go to the Vigil."

"Okay," Pam interjected before Will could go on, "I just want to check something … You called *him,* right? And asked to meet with him as soon as possible?" She looked at Will as if over the top of glasses on her nose. "You didn't know before you called that he was already planning to be here?"

She waited as if she expected a response. Will returned Pam's look and said slowly, "Right …"

Pam nodded, satisfied. "So is it Spencer's fault that you have to meet with him this weekend? Seems to me he's done what you wanted – he agreed to meet with you 'as soon as possible.' Right?"

Will's reluctant nod was slow in coming. He studied the patch of textured carpet between his feet for a moment or two. "So are you on Spencer's side now?" he finally asked, looking up at Pam as if he were a sheepish student.

She raised her eyebrows at him, accepting his tacit apology. "No way," she assured him, "but if he's not in the wrong, he shouldn't be blamed. No matter how much we don't like him, we are fair people."

"You're right. As always. And I think you and Abby must be in cahoots."

"Why is that?"

"She suggested I look at it the same way she's going to try to," Will explained. "She's not at all happy either, but she reminded me that she always has to make her plans contingent on the possibility of medical emergencies. She never knows when she might get called to the clinic or the hospital, even in the middle of church. She's going to think of this whole thing with Spencer as an emergency ... which in a way it is. So I guess I can try to do that, too."

"That's a good way to look at it," Pam agreed. "I like that."

"Me, too. I tell you," he said with an exaggerated sigh as he got up to go back into his office, "between the two of you, you're going to make sure I don't make an ass of myself, aren't you? But since when did you become such a good devil's advocate?"

88

"I always have been!" she reminded him. "It's just not usually directed at you."

"True dat, as the kids say. I'll try to keep that in mind." Will turned back to look at Pam. "Seriously, though, thank you for keeping me on track."

She smiled back at him. "You're welcome, boss. Anytime."

***

Only the trees and the birds knew the bones were still waiting under the snow, and they were as silent as the new flakes falling around and about them. They were the only ones who watched as some of the young maple saplings on the edge of the grove on the knoll bowed down on this Good Friday.

Chapter Eleven

Promises

The worst of the lunchtime rush was over and, as almost all the through-travelers cleared out, the locals started to come in. Since the diner was always closed for Easter, some of the regulars had developed the habit, years ago, of dropping by the day before to visit with friends they might not see the next, as they would most other Sundays. It didn't take long before a tradition was born, and soon almost everyone in town took part in the informal gathering every year.

This afternoon a few folks were absent since Passover had started the night before, and some were traveling, but there were still enough people to make for a spirited crowd in the big dining room. Booths and tables quickly filled up, and foot traffic was busy to and from the three buffet tables Gina had set up along the wall closest to the kitchen. Mary and Flora kept the coffee and hot water carafes filled, and Gina took care of the food.

While she waited to clear off a nearby table, Flora noticed that both Gina and Mary had placed their order pads near the cash register. "Won't you need those?" she asked Mary.

"Not unless a non-local comes in," Mary said, rinsing out an empty coffee pot. Once she'd started another pot to brew, she explained quietly. "See those spring baskets on all the tables? They're not just for decoration. Gina puts those out for contributions instead of charging

90

for the food. Those who can do so put in a few dollars, and most people do. Once in a while someone can't for some reason, but no one has to know and this way everyone can enjoy themselves."

She turned back to the big industrial coffee maker and continued as she filled up two glass pots. "It's one of the ways Gina says 'thank you' to the community. She says the donations always equal or surpass the cost of the food. Everyone's aware that she donates the proceeds to a group or need in town, so folks are usually pretty generous. Don't tell her that you know now, though," Mary whispered with a smile. "She always does it anonymously, but you know how small towns are … that kind of news gets around pretty fast, and all the regulars have known for years."

Flora took her own order pad out of her apron pocket and added it to the other two on the counter. She looked around the diner, at the now-empty stools in front of her, towards the dining room bustling with conversation and activity, and she watched Gina with the customers. *Every single one of them is her friend,* Flora realized. *I hope I can say that at some point.*

As if reading her thoughts, Gina came over to stand beside Flora. "Recognizing folks yet?"

"Actually, I am," Flora answered. "I don't remember names yet – I still have to ask who they are so I can get their coffee mugs – but I know that'll come."

"This is only your third day," Gina said, "so I think it's good you can recognize anyone so soon. Especially in such a crowd. It won't be long before you know who drives what kind of vehicle."

Flora laughed and said, "I've already figured out that it's a safe bet that muddy Subarus and pickup trucks equal local folks."

"Pretty much!" Gina pointed toward the front window. "And here come a couple more. I was wondering when they'd show up," she added.

By the time Abby, Elnora, Cindy and Charlie Taylor, and KT came in, Gina and Flora had all their filled coffee mugs and one butterfly-etched glass waiting on one of the two booth tables that remained empty.

"Anyone else coming?" Gina asked once everyone was seated. "You're missing a few folks – should I reserve this other table?"

Cindy nodded as she picked up her mug. "At least four more are on their way. Will's picking up Sherman, Bud, and Jeff, and they should be here soon."

"Okay. Flora, can you get one of the 'reserved' signs from under the register, please?" Gina looked at her watch, then said to Mary as she walked by, "Let's get their mugs on that table, too, please. We have just an hour before we meet with Spencer."

"Oh good," Abby said, "you're going, too, Gina?"

"Absolutely. I wouldn't miss it."

Mary came up with the four empty mugs in her hands and announced, as she distributed them on the table and looked out a window to the parking lot, "Will's driving in now, and Bud's right behind him."

An hour and ten minutes later, the young man at the desk was taken aback by the large group of people coming through the wide double-doored front entrance of the Pillars Inn. He quickly checked the guest register to see if he'd missed some reservations, and then he saw Will coming toward him while the others stayed in the foyer.

Will held up a hand in greeting. "Don't worry, Mike," he said, amused at the clerk's expression, "we're not here to check in. We've got an appointment with one of your guests in a few minutes. Would you let Matthew Spencer know we're here, please?"

While they waited, Will and the others moved to the parlor to the right of the foyer. This had obviously been the large living room of the old Georgian mansion that was still one of the anchors of Main Street and the center of town. Soon Spencer and another man appeared on the stairs. Will walked over to them as they reached the lobby, said a few words, and gestured toward the other room.

When Spencer reached the parlor doorway and saw the group of ten townspeople sitting on the couches and chairs, he looked first at his companion and then Will in surprise.

"What the hell is this?" he managed to say softly, albeit through gritted teeth. "I thought it was going to be just you and the lawyer."

"I never said that," Will reminded him, "but in any case, my friends are here as well because we all feel the same way." He pulled two more chairs into the circle the others had formed with the furniture. "What one of us says, we all say. I can assure you that none of us bites, so please join us and let's get started."

93

Sherman stood up and came forward, his hand extended to Spencer and the other man, introducing himself. Somewhat hesitantly, Matthew shook his hand and introduced David Perlman.

The niceties out of the way, Sherm said, "Don't blame Will, Mr. Spencer. He didn't know until this morning that he'd have company. We decided as a group that we wanted to join him, in part because we have some news that will affect your proposition."

"In what way?" Spencer asked as he and David Perlman finally sat down.

Both Abby and Gina, on either side of Elnora, started to speak, but the attorney interrupted them.

"If I may ... We need to deal with something else first, Mr. Spencer."

"And that is?"

"You have made it clear that you intend to develop land here in Arlington – in particular, 75 acres that is on land that belongs to Mrs. Elnora Rushlow. As we understand it, though, you have yet to make her an official offer. Mrs. Rushlow showed me a letter that you wrote and sent to her last summer. In that letter, which I have here, you said you were going to seize her property through eminent domain – even though it was not for sale, I need to add – but you failed to mention a specific amount."

Sherman stopped and looked at Spencer in silence for a moment, and then he indicated Elnora. "I also understand that you have yet to meet Mrs. Rushlow in person. Neither have you spoken with her, nor have you followed up on your letter, except with the Select Board.

Well," he continued, "this is Mrs. Rushlow. If you're serious about going forward on your proposal, now seems like a good time to make her that offer."

Perlman turned in his chair to stare at Spencer in astonishment. "You haven't made an offer yet? You led us to believe everything was already in process, that it was almost a done deal!"

"It *is* in process," Spencer countered, not looking at his client. "I've been waiting on the re-vote and it just seems like the Board keeps putting it off." He hesitated, as if steeling himself. "But I do intend to make an offer, and I'll do so now … but I'll write it down," he finished, making a gesture in the air with his hand, as if that would accomplish something.

"That's fine," Sherman agreed. "Here, I have some paper," he added, handing him a small steno pad.

In the silence that fell among them, Matthew thought for a minute and then wrote some figures on the pad. He got up and gave it to Elnora without a word, his eyes lowered. She, along with Gina and Abby, studied first Matthew and then the numbers. After she turned the pad back over to Sherman Weeks, she took hold of a hand of each of the women beside her.

Sherman looked at the amount, raised an eyebrow, and said, "Three hundred fifty thousand for over 70 acres? That's only $5000 an acre. As I'm sure you're aware, Mr. Spencer, that is *well* below market price. Nor is it fair for Mrs. Rushlow.

"That's for sure," Perlman said before Matthew could respond. "He's asking us for a hell of a lot more!"

Though no one looked at Spencer directly, everyone could see he was trying hard not to squirm in his chair. His face had turned red when Perlman spoke, but it was impossible to tell if it was from anger or embarrassment.

Probably a little of both, Sherman thought to himself, and he tried to ease the tension in the room. "Before you get more upset, Mr. Perlman," he said, looking steadily at the two men in turn, "and before you do, Matthew, you need to know that you are going to receive a counter-offer."

Spencer finally looked up. "A counter-offer? How is that possible?"

"As the attorney for the Arlington Farmers and Community Cooperative," Sherman said in his best professional voice, trying not to look pleased, "I can tell you that all these people here with me are going to give you some real competition."

Gina couldn't help herself and burst out with "You're damn right we are!"

"What do you mean, 'how is that possible'?" Bud asked, speaking up for the first time. "The only official papers you've filed with the town are your initial proposal to the Select Board, and that was months ago. Since then we have organized and worked to keep you from destroying important farmland. And today, on behalf of the Co-op and the town, we have officially notified Mrs. Rushlow that we want to make an offer on that property so that it will stay open land. That's how it's possible, Mr. Spencer."

"And," Gina said as she turned to Elnora and put a thick envelope in her hand, "it just so happens that I have here a little over $275 to offer you as earnest money."

"That's not nearly enough for earnest money!" Matthew exclaimed. "It has to be at least ten percent of the asking price."

Sherman folded his hands as he looked at Spencer. "Normally that's true, or some other percentage agreed upon by the two parties. But since there is no official figure to begin with, and since you've not offered any earnest money along with your proposal, I think," he said, looking around at the others, "that $275 is plenty in this case."

Spencer stood up and motioned for Perlman to do the same. He'd had enough. Still not looking at Elnora and ignoring the rest of the group, Spencer declared to Sherman Weeks, "You've not heard the last of me. My attorney will be in touch with you next week."

"I hope so," Sherman said, standing now, too.

Matthew held Sherm's steady gaze for a moment and looked like he was about to say something else. Instead he turned on his heels and David Perlman followed him. As soon as they reached the lobby, the group in the parlor could hear Perlman say, "We need to talk, Spencer."

They watched the two men ascend the staircase, Perlman still talking, his voice rising almost with every step. Spencer said nothing. A moment or two later, though, they heard a door slam, and the echoes of the ensuing argument drifted down into the parlor.

Chapter Twelve

Standing Vigil

A few minutes later, everyone filed down the front steps of the inn and into the late afternoon sun that streamed low along Battenkill Road to its intersection with Main Street. Bud and Elnora brought up the rear, Bud helping her slowly down the steps and the walkway to the parking lot. He made sure Elnora was comfortably settled in the passenger seat of his aging maroon Toyota Tacoma pickup truck and then sought out Abby and Will.

"I'll take Elnora home," Bud said. "I'd like to do a little ceremony near the sugarbush, and she said it was okay, so I'll drop her off first and then walk over."

"Sure, Bud. Thanks," Abby said. "Hope it goes well."

Will slapped his friend on the back and added, "Thanks for your help today, brother."

Bud's head and shoulders dipped almost into a slight bow before he smiled and turned back to his truck. His vehicle was the first to leave the parking lot.

Within half an hour, Bud was walking toward the ten-acre sugarbush on the far eastern side of the Rushlow property. A heavy blanket was slung across his left shoulder, and he held a large electric torch in one hand and a bundle of sage and a frame drum in the other.

The afternoon light was fast giving way to dusk, the temperature was falling again as the clouds continued to dissipate, and a sliver of the full Paschal moon was just coming into view over Stratton Mountain in the distance across from the highway. In between the farm and the highway, the waters of the Lye Brook wetlands and the heron rookery were starting to open up, and the wind-driven low waves reflected the scudding clouds overhead.

From his vantage point at the back edge of the trees above the WMA, Bud could just see the beaver lodge on this side of the highway, and the duck boxes that stood like sentinels above the dark water.

It was still a little too early for waterfowl or the herons to return to their nests, but Bud could see there had been some repair activity on the beaver lodge already. Several newly-hewn birch and poplar saplings sparkled white and gold in the rising moonlight, as if rings had been dropped atop the domed woodpile, and Bud stood still, waiting to hear if the signal *slap!* of the beavers' tails on the water would announce their presence.

After a while he decided it was too dark to hear or see anything else, so Bud found a snow-covered hummock of long grass and rutted soil, spread and knelt down on the blanket, put aside the torch, and placed the sage in the center. He picked up his deerskin-covered drum, held it up in the air as if in a salute, gently kissed the hide, and began to stroke it quietly with the hide-covered drumstick. The higher the moon rose over the mountain ridge across from him, the wetlands, and the sugarbush, the louder the drum sounded. Except for an occasional car driving past up on the road, no other sound was heard. Even the wind gradually died down as the moon rose higher and higher.

Still on his knees, Bud closed his eyes and started a slow chant as he drummed, so soft at first that only the trees and the leftover snowflakes in the air could hear him. Slowly the volume increased, as did the pace of his drumming, along with the moon's ascendance. Just as the bottom sliver of moon escaped the hold of the highest ridge, Bud got back on his feet and waited.

Soon the moon was high enough to cast shadows among the trees. Once the shadows reached him, Bud exchanged the drum for the sage bundle. He lit the sage, inhaling its penetrating fragrance, and smudged himself, the blanket, the drum. Intoning a prayer of thanksgiving to the Grandmothers and Grandfathers, and calling on the spirits of the trees to protect those among whom he stood, he extended the smoldering sage and his ongoing prayer to each of the four cardinal directions.

In the gathering moonlight, Bud finished his prayer with the solemn words of his ancestors. "'Of the East may the Great Spirit and the Great Creator bless us and smile upon us. *Knikinik volcanda kottiwi kwahliwi tapsiwi.'"* And a breeze picked up again, as if to carry his prayer to all the ends of the earth.

At the same time Bud was immersed in his ceremony, Abby walked into the almost-dark nave of the Episcopal Church three or four miles away. Because it was the service of the Easter Vigil, the first Eucharist of Easter, all artificial lighting was muted at first. The closer to sunset it got, some unseen person used the silent rheostat to dim the electric sconces on the stone walls little by little as the minutes went by.

She could hear other people coming in, and the whispers of the officiants as they finished their preparations, but she had purposefully tucked herself into a far corner of the pews so she couldn't see anyone. Tonight especially Abby welcomed the deep quiet of the worship space as it grew increasingly darker. This was her favorite service of the liturgical year and, given all the recent activity, phone calls, and conversations around the new Co-op – to say nothing of her regular work at the clinic – she felt the need to prepare alone and in silence.

Gradually the pews filled up and slowly the congregation fell quiet. Suddenly all the lights were fully extinguished and the nave was completely dark. Abby could almost hear a collective sharp indrawn breath all around her. She knew what was coming and she smiled a little to herself as she stood and turned to the back of the nave and waited.

Into the expectant hush the sharp sound of flint against stone brought a flash of fire into the darkness, and the congregation turned as one to see the flame. Now, by its light, they could see the dim figures of the priest, two young acolytes on either side of her, and Will and a thurifer behind her, all vested in white, in a group around the large granite baptismal font. Will held a tall white Paschal candle in his hands and the acolytes each held a long, slim brass taper.

As if to let the congregation feast their eyes, the priest waited a moment. Then she addressed the people, all of whom were now standing.

"'Dear friends in Christ: On this most holy night, in which our Lord Jesus passed over from death to life, the

Church invites her members, dispersed throughout the world, to gather in vigil and prayer. For this is the Passover of the Lord, in which, by hearing his Word and celebrating his Sacraments, we share in his victory over death.

"'Let us pray.

"'O God, through your Son you have bestowed upon your people the brightness of your light. Sanctify this new fire," the priest continued, her hand held out to the flame, "and grant that in this Paschal feast we may so burn with heavenly desires, that with pure minds we may attain to the festival of everlasting light ...'"

At a nod from the priest, one of the acolytes held his taper over the new fire and the unburned wick flamed to life. First he reached up to put the lighted taper to the Paschal candle and then to the other acolyte's taper. The two acolytes turned to the priest and the other officiants and, in turn, lit the small candles they each held, cupped in a small square of cardboard to catch the hot drips of wax.

The priest's voice now lifted into the silence as she began to sing the Exsultet *á cappella,* and the procession began to move forward. The acolytes led the way through the nave, stopping at each pew on their respective sides to light the small candles the first person held out to them. Slowly the body of the church filled with small glittering flames as all of the congregation's candles were lighted.

When the procession reached the steps of the chancel, Will placed the Paschal candle in its stand next to the lectern, and the priest stood next to it as she continued the hymn. "' ... How holy is this night ...'" she sang, "'How blessed is this night when earth and heaven are joined and [humankind] is reconciled to God ...'"

102

At her final 'Amen,' the priest, officiants, and acolytes moved up into the sanctuary, and the priest announced, "'Let us hear the record of God's saving deeds in history ...'" She, the officiants, and all the congregation sat as the Liturgy of the Word began. Individuals from the pews came one at a time to the lectern and read assigned scripture and psaltery passages from the Hebrew Covenant.

Abby was the sixth reader. By the light of the Paschal candle, she recited the story in the Book of Ezekiel of the valley of the dry bones. For some reason, the passage held her interest more than usual tonight. She returned to her seat in the back of the nave slowly, trying to discern the reason for its unusual hold on her.

One more reader followed Abby and the people sang a canticle to close the Liturgy of the Word. The service continued through the baptismal vows, and Abby continued to ponder the words of the passage, only responding by rote at the appropriate times.

Finally the moment they were all waiting for arrived and Abby forced herself out of her reverie. After a moment of silence, the priest sang out words that had not been heard for six weeks. "'Alleluia. Christ is risen.'" The congregation replied, "'The Lord is risen indeed. Alleluia.'" And all the lights came back on at once, the church bell ringing out for all the town to hear.

As one of the acolytes went to the Paschal candle, lighted his taper, and moved to the altar to light the candles there, the priest spooned incense into the glowing embers in the censer. The thurifer closed the top as the fragrant smoke emerged and enveloped the sanctuary and then the nave.

The church bell continued for a full minute, and four miles away, Bud stopped his chant to listen, letting the joyous sound become one with his song. A short while later, the liturgy ended, the bell pealed again, and the church doors opened.

As Bud began his own ancient hymn again, he thought he heard something in the air around him. He tried to listen beyond the music of the church bell that joined his song, but he heard nothing more, and the song and the bell swelled into a chorus. He looked up at the moon, and in its light he could see the tendrils of the smoking sage and the incense from the censer meet on the breeze across the miles and rise into the air like a prayer.

"Let it be so," Bud whispered, kneeling on the blanket.

"Amen," Abby said softly to herself as she walked out and down the steps into the moon-flooded night.

Chapter Thirteen

Connections

"Well, I know you went to church this weekend," KT said to Abby as Abby came into the office of the clinic and switched her jacket for her white lab coat.

"I sure did," Abby said. "How can you tell?"

"You still smell like incense," KT responded with a smile, handing her a patient file.

"Oh, good. One reason I like the 'high holy' liturgies is that the incense stays with me for a while." Abby thought a moment and then mused, "It's like a reminder, you know?"

KT studied Abby and then nodded. "It seems like something special happened this time," she ventured. "Something different ..."

"Not really. Well, yes and no. There were no lightning bolts, certainly," Abby started, "but for some reason I can't stop thinking about Elnora's land ... and that's all I thought about during the liturgy Saturday night," she finished in a rush. "I couldn't concentrate. I still feel like I'm in a fog ... like the incense took me somewhere into the clouds."

"Wow. I'd say something profound was – and still is – going on. Maybe," KT suggested, "you have to live with that feeling for a while. Something or someone will bring things into focus eventually."

Abby looked at KT with a fond smile. "You're pretty wise for your age, you know. Thanks for listening. And for the advice. You're right, of course. I'd love to talk it out some more, but," she added, visibly bringing herself back to the present, "I can't keep our patients waiting. Tell me about this first one." Abby looked through the thin file folder. "This is her first visit, but the name is familiar."

"Flora MacDonald. You've met her. She's on the waitstaff now at Gina's place, and she was at Town Meeting."

"Oh, right. She's the tall attractive gal with the dark auburn hair, the one who moved here recently and I thought worked for Spencer."

"Yep. She called a couple of weeks ago for an appointment. She wants to get established with a doctor, and Gina recommended you. And look," KT added, pointing to a line near the top of the first page in the file, "she lives pretty close to me. She's on Mill Pond Road."

"How 'bout that?" Abby said, beaming at KT. "You can visit back and forth."

"That would be fine," KT agreed. "She's only a couple of years older than I am."

Abby looked at the clock on the wall and buttoned up her lab coat. "Well, I guess it's time to get my head out of the clouds and get to work," she said as she moved to the hallway door. "I look forward to meeting her."

"I think you'll like her. I met her on one of her first days at Gina's, and she seems real nice. In fact, I've been wondering …"

Abby turned around, waiting for KT to finish.

"Do you think I could invite Flora to a meeting about the Co-op?" she asked. "It'd be a good way for her to meet folks."

"That's a wonderful idea. It's not a secret group, and we'll have to go public soon, anyway. See if she wants to come to the meeting on Wednesday. We'll be at Gina's for dinner. It's Will's favorite night – her mac and cheese is the special."

"It was probably his suggestion, then," KT laughed and Abby nodded with a knowing grin. "Thanks. I'll see Flora tomorrow at Gina's and ask her then."

"Sounds good. And now," Abby said, "it really is time to get to work!"

"Yes, ma'am," KT replied with a salute. "I'll take Flora to Room 3."

A few minutes later, Abby knocked softly on the exam room door and entered. "Good morning, Ms. MacDonald. I'm Dr. Abby Phillips. It's nice to finally meet you."

Flora stood when Abby walked in. "Thank you – you, too. Please, call me Flora."

"Thank you, Flora." Abby sat down on the rolling stool and Flora sat back in the one chair in the room, her hands folded in her lap.

"Well," Abby said, looking at the chart and then at Flora, "I imagine you must have a bit of Scots blood in you, with your surname. Most of my own heritage is Welsh, but

I have a fair amount of Scots as well. Do you ever wear your plaid?"

"I would, but there are a lot of different MacDonald clans and I don't know which one – or ones – to claim."

Abby nodded as she rolled over to the computer on a small black steel table. "If I explored that part of my lineage, I'd have the same trouble. Frasers seem to have a few groupings, too, and I haven't a clue how or where to start looking."

She turned to the computer, found Flora's medical record and files from Montpelier, and took a moment to read over the synopsis KT had provided. She looked at Flora and said, "Everything looks good from these. Do you have any complaints or anything you want me to pay special attention to?"

Flora shook her head. "No, nothing. I'm doing all right. I just thought I should establish myself here."

"That's a good idea. Let me check you over so we have a baseline, then, and we'll set up another appointment in six months. If everything's good then, we'll start a yearly schedule."

"Sounds good. Thanks, Dr. Phillips."

Abby nodded again. "In the meantime, if you ever have any concerns, call anytime, and KT will fit you in right away." She stood and motioned for Flora to sit on the paper-covered exam table. "And speaking of KT," Abby added some moments later, briefly going out of her doctor mode, "she's got a proposal for you that I hope you'll consider."

"Okay," Flora said, looking at Abby, seated on the stool again, the exam complete.

When Abby saw Flora's quizzical expression, she said, "I'll let her explain. I do hope you'll think about it, though. So," she finished her tone lighthearted as she closed the computer and Flora's file, "if all goes well, I'll see you back here in six months, and out and about in town before that."

"I'm looking forward to that," Flora answered.

"Me, too. And welcome to town."

Chapter Fourteen

Home is ...

KT sat on the sunny side of the small booth, enjoying the welcome warmth and her iced coffee that Flora brought over as soon as she sat down. Even though it was her day off, a ballpoint pen was stowed away at the top of KT's thick ponytail as usual, and the bright sun glinted off the pen's chrome cap and the red highlights in her hair, creating something of an aura of Christmas tree lights around her head.

The Capital Diner wasn't busy yet, so when Flora put her eggs benedict on the table, KT asked if she could sit down for a few minutes. Flora looked around to make sure the few patrons were taken care of and said, "It looks like I can take a short break. Thanks."

"It was good to see you yesterday," KT said, cutting into her egg-and Hollandaise-covered English muffin. "How'd you like Abby?"

"I like her a lot. She seems real nice. She even took the time to talk a little about her Scots background, so we talked some about that." Flora sat back in the booth. "She also said you have something you want to ask me?"

KT put down her cutlery and sat back, too. "Yes, actually. I've been thinking about this for a couple of weeks now and checked with Abby. I'm wondering if you'd be interested in joining a group we're involved with ..."

"The one that meets here so often?"

"That's the one," KT nodded. "You saw and heard some of them at Town Meeting, the group with the 'Save the Herons' signs. We've grown a little since then, and we've formed into a non-profit co-op of farmers and supporters to keep Elnora Rushlow's farm safe from development by Matthew Spencer." She picked up her utensils again and added, "I thought you might like to come to a meeting, meet the folks, and maybe get involved."

Flora's response was immediate. "I'd love to, if I have the time. Anything to save any part of the environment, especially farmland and wetlands. I'm still working two jobs, though."

"I have the same time constraints," KT assured her, "and understand perfectly. Come to the meeting tomorrow if you can, though, and meet everyone. Any way we can support the work is welcome, however small."

"I can do that, depending on the time. Will you meet here?"

KT shook her head. "We're meeting at Elnora's around 6:30 or 7:00. Whenever folks get there, actually," she chuckled. "We're kind of loose. I'll be glad to pick you up – it might be easier than trying to explain the directions."

"Sounds great," Flora said, standing up as she prepared to go back to work. "I'll write down my address and phone number before you leave. Thanks for asking me."

"Excellent! Is 6:15 okay to pick you up? That way we'll get there early enough for you to meet a few people before the crowd arrives."

Several hours later, KT drew up to Flora's house in a cul-de-sac of the Mill Pond Mobile Home Park off East Street. The old gristmill – the one built in 1764 by Remember Baker, the first town clerk and first cousin of Ethan Allen – for which the park was named had been refurbished as a museum in recent years and stood on a small hill where most of the residents could see its sturdy frame. A landscaped postage stamp park spanned a tributary of the Battenkill that fed into and out of the pond, and children were playing on the swings and the basketball court. Across the street from the mill, the former train depot had been similarly rehabilitated and now housed artists' studios, incubator groups, and a small florist.

Flora's beige and white singlewide trailer faced due west across from a five-acre parcel of oak, copper beech, birch, maple, and hemlock woods. As KT walked up the gravel driveway, she noticed a metalcrafted 'Welcome' sign on a short steel post that included the words 'Home is Where Your Story Begins.' Songbirds flew to and from a couple of birdfeeders on the brown-stained front porch, even as KT climbed the four stairs and raised her hand to knock on the door.

Before she could, Flora opened it and invited KT inside. "Hope you don't mind cats," Flora noted as a large tabby and a small calico greeted KT by rubbing around her ankles before she could take more than a couple of steps into the living room. "I should've thought to ask you this morning."

KT laughed and said, "I've got two myself, so yours probably smell mine."

"Ah ha. Then you'll get the once-over again when you go home," Flora said, showing KT to a small recliner.

"That's for sure." KT leaned over and stroked the two cats as they took turns trying to jump into her lap. "I wish mine were this friendly with strangers."

Flora sat on the edge of the couch across from KT. "They usually aren't at all," she said, shaking her head. "They obviously know you're a cat person. Usually they hide in the back room when new people come in."

"If you ever need someone to take care of them if you go away, I'm available."

"Thanks, KT! I usually don't go anywhere long enough for that, but maybe now I can think about taking a short trip. I appreciate that. And I can reciprocate in kind."

"Anytime. I'd be glad to."

"Well," Flora said as she stood up, "let me go switch my slippers for my shoes and then we can go, if you're ready."

"I'm ready. That'll get us there in plenty of time."

While Flora was in her bedroom, KT looked around the small living room as she continued to stroke the cats. She noticed an old-looking portrait on the pale yellow wall between a window and the door. The oval oil painting of a curly-haired baby, depicted from the shoulders up, was set into a wide square and gilded frame of old cracked wood.

"What a beautiful child!" she exclaimed as soon as Flora reappeared.

Flora turned to where KT was looking and smiled. "Isn't she gorgeous? That's Emily, my late great-great aunt on my father's side of the family. She was about six months old when the portrait was done. Unfortunately she died soon afterward."

Still entranced by the painting, KT said nothing for a moment. "How sad," she said as she finally reached for her keys on the table next to the recliner and looked at Flora, "but at least her parents had this to remember her by."

"Yes. And, so the story goes, they also named their next child – also a girl – in her memory. Apparently I actually met the second Emily once when I was young, but I don't remember the occasion."

"Wow, what a story ..."

Flora waited until they were both in KT's Impreza before she responded. "It is a fascinating story. I think it is, anyway. Aunt Emily – the second one – was an early feminist, a writer, and she taught young women at a school in the Berkshires she and her older sister, Lillian, founded. As my brother and I grew up, she wrote us long letters and was thrilled when she found out I had started to write poetry. Neither of the sisters married, so I think Emily kind of felt we were her adopted children."

"You're a poet? That's very cool," KT said. "You and Bud have something in common, then."

"I don't know that I'm really a poet. I've written some poems in the past, and I read poetry sometimes, but it's been a couple of years since I've written anything. I didn't know that about Bud," Flora added. "Has he been published?"

KT reached the stop sign at the bottom of East Street and turned left onto Main Street before she responded. "He has, a few times – and he's really quite good, I think. I'm not a poet by any stretch, but I like what I read of his. According to Will, who's a writer himself, Bud's got poems in some well-known publications."

Adjusting in her seat so she could see KT better, Flora asked, "With such talent in town, is there a writers' group, by any chance?"

"Not that I know of, but you can ask Bud or Will tonight. There is the writing program that Bennington College is famous for, and that's not far from here at all. If there isn't anything in town, though, maybe you all can start up a group."

"I'd really like that." Flora's voice trailed off as she looked out the passenger side window. After a few minutes of watching the trees and farms and melting snow go by as they drove, she turned again to face KT.

"So tell me some more about this heron group that turned into a farmers' co-op," she said. "That's an interesting change."

Matthew Spencer spent most of Tuesday evening at his office because he didn't want to go home. Even as it grew slowly darker, he sat in his desk chair staring out the window onto the fast-emptying parking lot.

From his vantage point in the middle of the first floor of the last building in this little city of offices, he watched the traffic increase up on Corporate Woods Boulevard. It was too early for any of the cleaning company crews to arrive, so soon his Escalade, parked directly across from his window, was one of only a handful of vehicles that remained in the front part of the lot that he could see.

At first he told himself, and Sonia and Jacob as they left for the day, that he didn't want to fight the rush hour congestion. The longer he sat, though, the more Matthew thought about his Saturday night encounter with those people in Arlington and the more his agitation increased. He was restless but he couldn't make himself move.

Once it was dark enough that all he could see were streams of headlights and brakelights heading to and from Albany, Matthew swiveled his chair back around to the desk. For lack of anything better to do, he picked up one of his business cards and looked at it. He never considered the irony of such a fancy embossed statement sitting there for the taking on his simple, utilitarian steel desk in the confines of his small two-room office because he always made sure to meet potential clients at restaurants or their places of business.

The problem was, he thought, turning the card over and over in his hands, he had no clients at the moment. He hadn't told his associates yet, but Perlman had gone back to New Jersey in a snit Saturday night. Matthew had called several times and left messages, but he'd received no response.

He'd try an email when he got home, after he replied to Eric Thompson's note from this morning that said his wife had a friend who was interested in the property, too. And tomorrow, he reminded himself, he had to talk with his attorney before Weeks did.

Matthew heaved a big sigh, pushed his chair back, and stood up. He put the business card back in its chrome and acrylic stand, got his keys from the middle desk drawer. His eyes shifted left to the two encased shelves that held his high school and college athletic trophies. Baseball and basketball scholarships had helped him get through the University of Albany, and he thought back to his first client, a former teammate who had 'made it' in politics.

If only things were as easy now as they had been when he was that young athlete and college graduate, he thought, picking up the largest trophy from his senior as a Great Dane at Albany. He studied it for a few moments, as though the names of his old connections and new possibilities would jump out at him.

It wasn't all that many years ago, he told himself. Maybe he should go to his twelfth reunion, after all. It was still six months away, and he didn't want to risk seeing the football coach who had given him such grief, but maybe it would help generate some more clients.

Finally Matthew replaced the trophy gently, turned off the lights in his office and the outer room, and then locked the corridor door that had his name on the frosted glass. The Escalade was the only car left in the lot. If he had bothered to look up, he'd have seen that a few stars were visible through the still-budding tree branches.

The drive east to Center Brunswick was uneventful. Since he'd not had to wait through rush hour, his time on the road took about twenty minutes, much less than the usual hour-long misery. If he'd driven the speed limit, it would have taken about thirty minutes – though he did wonder why he was in such a hurry to get home – so he was glad there was no police presence along the way. The last thing he needed was another speeding ticket.

His parents' house, a dusky grey three-bedroom ranch set farther back from the street than those of the neighbors, was hard to see at night when no lights were on. Matthew had forgotten to leave on the front porch light. Because the long stretch of strip malls on NY Route 7 was two or three streets away, the glare of consumerism didn't reach to his driveway, but he'd grown up in this house and could make his way around with no problem.

Once inside, he switched on the desk lamp in the former den he used as his home office, checked to see if there were any messages on the answering machine that only his parents used now, and sat down and turned on the desktop computer. The rest of the house remained in darkness as he worked.

An hour or so later, he turned off the computer and the desk lamp and walked down the hall to his bedroom at the opposite end of the house. Matthew didn't even bother to turn on a light in his room as he changed to pajama bottoms, climbed into his unmade bed, and lay flat on his back as he tried to go to sleep.

Just as KT had predicted, Will and Bud had been glad to talk with Flora about their own creative work and writing in general, and the three of them had agreed to get together on occasion. Abby and KT had stood nearby, in the doorway of Elnora's kitchen, smiling as they listened to the three make plans for the following Sunday afternoon.

On the way back to Flora's, she and KT chattered like old friends, and KT accepted Flora's invitation to go in for a cup of herbal tea before she headed home herself. The two cats greeted KT as before, rubbing around her ankles and mewling at Flora as if they hadn't eaten in days. Soon they had all made themselves comfortable in the small living room, picking up on their earlier conversation. There were few lamps, but the light they shed was warm and cozy. Before the young women knew it, the hour grew late and they both decided they had to call it a night.

"You came into the diner so early, I know you didn't even sleep in this morning," Flora said, apologizing for keeping KT up so long. "I'm sorry I've been running my mouth – that's what happens when I get excited, but I'm so glad we've gotten to know each other better."

"Me, too," KT said, giving Flora a hug as she prepared to leave. "You've got some great things to look forward to now. You're a fabulous addition to the co-op group, and I know you'll enjoy writing with the boys."

Flora leaned against the doorjamb, reluctant to let the evening end. "I hope I can contribute something useful to both groups, but I *am* looking forward to participating in both. And maybe the guys can help me make some progress on the book I've been working on for four or five years."

119

She returned KT's hug as she said, "Thank you for making tonight possible."

"No problem. I can't wait to hear more about your novel when you come over Thursday night."

KT stopped on her way out and gave the portrait of Emily a slight nod and said, "Bye, Emily. Nice to meet you. You two take care of each other."

Chapter Fifteen

Twists and Turns

Traffic coming off of Route 7 from Exit 3 on its way to Rt. 7A passed Charlie Taylor in the white sedan he used when on duty as constable. He had parked in his usual place on the mile-long byway from the exit, tucked into the wide shoulder just around the curve beyond Mack Molding, and those who knew the car slowed their speed accordingly. Some drivers even waved at Charlie as they went past and he waved back.

Matthew Spencer wasn't that lucky.

He was on the phone with Sherman Weeks, to let him know he was on his way to the meeting they'd arranged yesterday, that he'd be there in a few minutes, when he looked in the rearview mirror to see the flashing blue lightbar on the roof of Charlie's car.

After a few choice words, which he didn't think to keep to himself, Matthew added that he'd be a little late now, stabbed the 'end' button without waiting for Sherman's response, and guided the Escalade over to the right shoulder.

Charlie appeared at the now-open driver's side window, his ticket book in hand. "Good morning, Mr. Spencer. Beautiful day we're having, eh?"

"Is it? I wouldn't know, especially now. And how the hell do you know my name?"

"Your vanity tags make it pretty clear," Charlie said, trying to keep his tone pleasant. "You have to admit we've seen your vehicle around town quite a bit, and it does kind of stand out."

Matthew nodded. "True. I'd forgotten the plates." He reached into the glove box and brought out his registration and insurance cards, and then he pulled his license out of his wallet and handed them all to Charlie. "Can we hurry this up? I'm already late for a meeting."

"This shouldn't take long, Mr. Spencer. I'm just going to give you a warning about your speed this time," Charlie said. "What I will cite you for, though, is talking on a cell phone." He leaned down a little to look into the window. "I would've thought you'd have a hands-free device in this car, especially since it's illegal in New York, too, to talk on the phone while you're driving."

"I do, but I left it at the office."

"Well, next time be sure to have it," Charlie said as he tore off the ticket and handed it to Spencer. "Or better yet, get two. That way you'll always have one in the car."

Matthew took the ticket without looking, along with the other items and his license, and put them all on the passenger seat. Charlie put his hand on the car door and added, "You have a good day now."

"Yeah, thanks," Matthew said as he started up the Escalade again. He waited for the constable to move away before he drove off, his thoughts already going to the meeting he needed to get to.

As often happens in April, summer temperatures settled in a few days after the last of the snow melted, and the ice went out on the waters of Lye Brook WMA and the heron rookery. Because of the sudden heat, mud season was already drying up, turning the rutted dirt roads into dusty vortices as vehicles made their way along them. The stronger sun prompted trees to bud, which put a definitive end to the sugaring season that had already slowed down. Harvesters made fewer trips to their sugarbushes now, and Elnora's small family crew was no exception.

Bud had arranged for some of the Academy students to join the last excursion of the season to check the taps and finish the final harvest. He and the students drove to the farm, put on their rubber boots, and they walked the long pathway through Elnora's yard and fields to the stand of century-old sugar maples.

Some of the teens collected the remainders of the sap run, while others gathered up the galvanized buckets that were empty, and still others closed and pulled taps from the trees. Jeff Bedell was responsible for cleaning up the deadfall, the largest of which would be prepared, dried, and stacked for next year's wood fires in the house and under the evaporator. Using a sturdy rake and a snow shovel, he made a trail of branch piles around the exterior of the grove.

As he worked his way back to the path, Jeff found himself on a small hummock of dead grasses and drying mud. He straightened up to rest a moment and look through the trees for a glimpse of the Lye Brook wetlands.

When he bent down to pick up the rake and the shovel, he noticed now-rigid tire tracks in the mud at his feet.

Jeff used the snow shovel to try to loosen the dirt around the tracks so the path would smooth out again. Every few steps, as he pushed into the soil – *Damn frost heaves*, he said softly – he hit what he thought was gravel. This was strange since there was little to no gravel – unusual in itself for Vermont soils – elsewhere along this particular field path.

He stopped digging and picked up a handful of dirt and gravel, letting his fingers serve as a sieve for the dirt. What remained in his hands was not gravel after all, but bones, bones that were too big to be from an animal.

***

Matthew didn't see him, but Will was on his way to Sherman Weeks' home office, too, and drove past at the same time Spencer had first pulled onto the shoulder, the constable right behind him.

Poor Matt, he muttered to himself, remembering Abby's account of Spencer's speed on Route 7A last month. *He's going to hate coming to town if this keeps up.*

"That's not necessarily a bad thing," Sherman suggested several minutes later when Will arrived at Weeks' home and told him what he'd seen and thought.

"Agreed. But I guess I'm enough of an optimist to hope he has a change of heart and won't get a bad taste in his mouth about us."

124

Sherman's amusement was apparent as he said, "I don't know if that makes you an optimist or naïve, my friend."

Will reached for the mug of coffee Sherm offered him and said over his shoulder as they went into the den-sized office, "Or maybe both."

"I can't argue with that," the attorney responded in a mock-serious tone. Just as they sat down on the comfortable corduroy-covered couch, the desk phone rang and Sherman jumped back up to answer.

"It's Bud," he announced, looking at the caller ID.

He said almost nothing as he listened to Bud, but Will was fascinated by the myriad changes of expression on his face. Finally Bud rang off and Sherm returned to the couch, picking up his own coffee for a sip or two before he said anything. "It seems we have another development in the saga of Matthew Spencer."

"What's going on?"

At that moment the doorbell rang and Sherman said, "I'll tell you in a minute – although if that's Spencer himself, I can tell you both at the same time."

Will could hear Matthew's raised voice before he came into the house. By the time he and Sherm reached the office, Spencer had moderated his volume somewhat, but the flush on his face betrayed his agitation. Or maybe it was from the explanation he'd offered Sherman as apology for his tardiness.

"Seems Mr. Spencer was caught up in road work delays," Sherm said to Will as they all found seats.

"A sure sign spring is on the way," Will responded with a solemn nod, "when the road construction starts again. Right, Matt?"

"Just something we have to put up with, I guess."

"Vermont's bad enough," Will said, "but Albany must be a real treat when they start working on the roads again."

"That's for sure," Matthew said, shifting so he sat back more comfortably on the couch. His flushed face was slowly returning to its normal color, his grey eyes didn't seem as strained as before, and his high forehead had lost some of its creases. "It's especially bad because so many streets are one way. Luckily I don't work in the city, though. Most of the way here is on Route 7 and that's not usually too bad."

Sherman couldn't resist. "Except for today," he said, not looking at Will.

"Right," Spencer acknowledged, avoiding the other men's eyes. "Except for today."

"Well, you're here now," Sherm said, "so let's get started."

Will held up a hand to get Weeks' attention. "Before you do, Sherm ..." He turned to face Spencer and said, "I have to drive to and from Albany a lot, so I'm familiar with Route 7. One thing that strikes me every time is how built up so much of that corridor is now. So many of the old farms and farmland are gone, developed into individual businesses – or, even worse, strip malls Sometimes it seems like they go up overnight, and I start worrying whenever I see a new 'For Sale' sign go up.

"So I'm curious, Matt," Will continued, picking up steam, "do you ever think of those things? Do you miss the open fields that are now housing developments or fast food restaurants or motorcycle shops or big box stores?"

"I never really thought about it," Matthew answered, shrugging his shoulders. "It's just the way things are today."

"There's even a new complex of condos in Troy," Will added, not letting Matt finish, "on that tiny island in the Hudson between the bridges that's surrounded by the highways! How can anyone live in a place like that? As nice as the place looks, the people must feel like sardines!"

Spencer nodded and looked like he was going to say something when Will jumped in again. "Did you have anything to do with that development, Matt?"

Now Matt shook his head and Will sat back with a sigh of relief.

"As I started to say," Matthew continued, "nowadays the easy money is in land. The old farmers are dying off, their children don't want to or can't keep up the farms, and the land has to be used somehow ..."

"Why?" Will demanded. "Why does the land *have* to be used? Why can't it be left open?"

Matt looked at Sherman, who responded, "You're welcome to argue with him. I'm not going to."

"What good does it do to leave it open?" Matthew asked Will. His tone of voice told the other men his question was sincere.

Sherm and Will looked at each other, nonplussed. Then Sherman, his eyes wide with revelation, leaned toward Matt. "You haven't known anything *but* development, have you, Mr. Spencer?"

Will's mouth fell open in a silent *Ah ha!* as Matthew said, "I don't know ... I guess not."

Weeks added, "Have you always lived in the Albany area?"

"All my life. And my parents, too, before they moved to Florida for part of the year. All of my family has."

Will and Sherman looked at each other again, this time with raised eyebrows in a mutual yet unspoken understanding. At Sherm's almost indistinguishable nod, Will asked softly, "Matt, would you like to know – really get to know – why we're so determined not to develop the Rushlow farm?"

Spencer was quiet for a moment as he studied the men on either side of him. He sensed something had changed, but he couldn't identify anything specific. He sat up straighter, took a deep breath, and said a simple, though hesitant, "Okay."

"Excellent," Will said. "We don't want to be your adversaries, Matt," he affirmed. "We really don't. We are committed to our cause, but I think now we might be able to come to an understanding that suits *all* of us."

"And," Sherm added, "maybe we can do so without the lawyers." He stood up and refilled all their coffee mugs. "Before we make any other plans, though, I need to tell you both about the phone call I had just before you arrived, Mr. Spencer."

"Oh, that's right," Will said.

Sherman sat back down, his coffee mug in hand, and looked at Matt. "Our friend Bud has been out at the Rushlow sugarbush with some of his students today. They're cleaning up from the winter and sugaring, and one of the students found something of interest."

Here he turned to Will and continued. "It seems young Mr. Bedell uncovered some bones. Human bones, apparently. And," Weeks finished, focusing on Matthew again, "they're underneath the tire tracks you left, Mr. Spencer, when you drove onto the property several weeks ago."

Will stood up to return his mug to the tray on which the coffee fixings sat, and asked, "Has Abby been called in? And Charlie?"

Sherm nodded. "Yes to both."

"How do they know the tracks are mine?" Spencer asked. "They could've come from anyone ..."

"That's unlikely," Sherman replied. "Your vehicle is the only one that's been on that pathway for months."

"How is that even possible? You said yourself there were people there today, and surely others have driven there before and after me."

Will answered this time, shaking his head. "Everyone else knows to walk to the sugarbush, Matt. The only conveyance anyone uses is Elnora's horse and sledge and that's only in the snow. So it had to be you."

"So what does that mean? Am I in trouble?"

"Not at this point, Mr. Spencer," Weeks said. "I presume Charlie has already called in the state police by now, and the medical examiner. They'll be the ones to make that determination. They'll probably contact you soon, but that doesn't mean you need to worry."

"We might hear from Abby or Bud first," Will suggested and Sherman agreed. They both watched as Matthew sat, elbows on knees, his head in his hands, shoulders drooped.

"Look," Sherm said, "unless you put those bones there, or the body they belong to – or know who did – you have no cause for alarm."

When Matthew still said nothing, the other two looked at each other.

"You didn't, did you, Matt?" Will asked, his question almost a demand.

Finally the younger man looked up and seemed to come back to the room around them. He shook his head just enough to show that he had heard Will and Sherman.

"No, I didn't," he declared softly.

"Then you've nothing to worry about," the lawyer said again. "The most you can be cited for is trespassing, and if that's all it is, I doubt Elnora will press charges. In the meantime, we'll just have to wait", Sherman added. "It seems we have a mystery on our hands, and that will need to be cleared up before you have any hope of going forward with development plans. I suggest, then, that you call your attorney, Mr. Spencer, and tell him what's happened. He can call me if he has any questions."

"If it's any reassurance," Will said, patting Matthew on the back, "this will give us plenty of time to introduce you to the co-op group. There's a meeting early next week, if you'd like to come."

Spencer stood up to leave. As he picked up his still-unopened portfolio case, he said, "Sure. If they'll still have me. It's worth a try, I guess."

"That's the spirit," Sherman said

He and Will shook hands with Matt and were surprised when Matthew's hand stayed in each of theirs a little longer than necessary.

Sherman nodded at Spencer. "We'll get this all sorted out, son. Don't you worry."

Chapter Sixteen

Soundings

Abby was almost through with her rounds at the hospital when Charlie called. He was still at the Rushlow farm and had already notified the county coroner, the state police, and the medical examiner.

"I can come, of course ... but do I really need to be there, since all the official folks are on their way?"

"Bud asked me to call you. I'm not sure why, but he practically insisted."

"Okay. I just want to look in on Wanda Jarvis," Abby told Charlie, "and then I'll meet you there. She had her heart procedure yesterday and I need to check on her."

"Hope she's doing okay. Cindy's been worried about her."

"She should be fine. It was just an angiogram, but we wanted to keep an eye on her to make sure, given her age and history. Her cardiologist is keeping me updated and KT saw her last night. Neither of them has said anything to be concerned about."

"That's good," Charlie said. "If you're allowed to, please let her know we're thinking of her."

"Will do. As soon as I'm through here, then, I'll head back to town. See you in a little while."

Bud met Abby as she walked out to the sugarbush from Elnora's house. A couple of hundred yards farther on, she could see Charlie and several other uniformed men and women standing in a rough circle that was marked off by yellow crime scene tape. Some of the Academy students were huddled along the edge of the bush, and one or two hovered near the law enforcement officials.

From the wetland behind them, the first red-winged blackbird of the season trilled his homecoming song.

"Hi, Abbs," Bud said as he gave her a hug. "Thanks for coming."

"Of course. Charlie said you wanted me here."

Bud's voice was so low – as if he thought the people behind him could hear – that Abby had to strain to hear him. "Because I know you'll understand. This isn't something I can say to just anyone."

Abby's raised eyebrows asked her question and her hand on Bud's arm encouraged him to continue when he stopped speaking. He moved to stand closer to Abby, both now facing the sugarbush.

"This may sound strange," Bud finally said, "but I think those bones are more important than anything to do with Spencer. Or anyone else, for that matter, at least recently."

"I don't understand …"

He shook his head with a rueful smile. "I'm not explaining this well, sorry."

Bud pointed to the yellow tape that delineated the exposed bones. "I don't think this is a crime scene. Of any kind, nefarious or accidental. Something tells me those bones are much older than that. I don't know what that 'something' is, exactly, and," he finished, pointing now to all the uniformed officials, "I don't know how to explain it to them, but … this place is different."

He shook his head again and held Abby's eyes in his gaze. "Something else is going on here."

As Abby studied Bud a moment, and thought through his words and demeanor, something niggled at the back of her mind, but she couldn't quite reach it. "Okay, my friend," she said finally, resting her hand once more on his arm. "I'll see what I can do."

After she squeezed his hand for further reassurance, Abby walked toward the others. Bud stayed where he was, looking in her direction but seemingly lost in a trance. Some of the students began to move in his direction, their voices quieting as they drew near and saw that actually he wasn't watching anyone at all.

"He's gone off to one of his places," someone whispered, and another turned to the rest of the group and held a finger to her lips. Nods of understanding passed along the line. They were used to this.

Abby wove in and out among the others who stood outside the yellow tape to draw up next to Charlie. When one of the officers' shoulder radio began to squawk, she stood on her tiptoes to whisper, "Bud doesn't think this is anything bad, that it's not a crime scene. What do you think?"

Charlie shrugged his shoulders and whispered back, "I can't tell, really, and they're not saying much to me. I think they probably don't know either, at this point."

"We'll find out more when the medical examiner gets here," Abby said in a normal tone of voice. "Any idea when she's due?"

"I heard one of the troopers say she's on her way, but that's all I know."

Abby looked behind her, to where Bud and the students were gathered, and back to Charlie. "Well, I guess we wait, then. Maybe we can go visit with Elnora for a ..."

The constable looked up when Abby stopped talking. She had halfway turned to start back when three figures appeared from around the corner of the old farmhouse, walking toward Bud's group. As they drew closer, Abby and Charlie could identify Will, Sherman, and Matthew Spencer.

Now Charlie muttered to Abby. "What the hell is he doing here?"

She didn't have to ask who he meant. "How could he possibly know?"

Charlie shook his head. "I had to give him a citation earlier today, though. It's a bit of a story," he said. "I'll tell you the details later, when he's not around, but I don't know why he's with Will and Sherm."

"For that matter, then," Abby added, "how do they know?"

By now the three men were on their way to join Abby and Charlie, and Bud followed them. Matthew

Spencer's pace slowed down visibly as they approached. Even as he hung back, Matt's gaze was focused a short distance in front of him to where three troopers stood just outside the crime scene tape. Two had their arms crossed as a third pointed at something on the ground inside the secured area and, without looking up, called over a fourth colleague. The latter bent down for a moment and then pulled out a pair of latex gloves to pick up a small item, which she placed into a glassine bag with care.

Abby saw Spencer watching the troopers and then take a few steps backward. She looked, too, at where the trooper was pointing and nudged Charlie to get his attention.

Just then her phone rang. "I've got to take this," she said, pulling out the cell phone and touching the screen. "It's the hospital – I hope it's not about Wanda."

Charlie nodded. "Go ahead. I'll stay here."

She moved a little way off so she could hear, and Bud and Will stopped nearby, giving her some room for privacy. Abby walked closer to them as she listened, a frown growing on her forehead. Coming to a stop next to her friends, she put her hand over the phone and said, "Can y'all tell Charlie I need to get back to the hospital? This is KT. She's checking in on Wanda. Looks like they need to start another procedure."

Abby concluded the call and looked at Bud. "Sorry, Bud. I'll be back as soon as I can," she said and hurried off in the direction of the Rushlow farmhouse and her car in the driveway.

The men knew she was worried because one of her 'Southernisms' had slipped into her words. Bud beckoned Charlie over and told him the news about Wanda. In turn, Charlie explained the small flurry of activity that had started while Abby was on the phone. Spencer inched closer as Charlie talked.

"One of the troopers found something embedded in the dry mud of the ruts," Charlie said, "so they've called in a forensics team. And the ME is almost here. She got off the highway a couple of minutes ago, apparently."

"Any idea what they found?" Will asked.

Charlie shook his head. "I don't know, Will. But at this point I couldn't say, even if I did."

"We'll find out soon enough," Sherm added, "or some of us will, anyway. I do believe the young lady who's coming our way may be the ME herself."

While they waited, Bud pulled Charlie aside and said, "I want to ask your advice about who I should talk to …"

"Sure, Bud."

"Abby knows this, which is why she was here … I guess I felt like I needed the moral support."

"What's going on?" Charlie asked, putting a hand on Bud's shoulder. "What's up?"

"I was here the night before Easter, in that very spot," Bud said, nodding to the taped-off area, around which the newly-arrived medical examiner now slowly circled. "There was still snow around – I made sure I stayed on the snowy spots because I made a small fire and

137

held ceremony – so I *know* there was snow on that clump of grass."

By now Charlie had taken out his small spiral flip notebook and was writing down Bud's observations. He looked up and said, "Of course it's all melted now because of the warmer temperatures, but was any mud showing that night?"

Bud nodded. "Some. Mostly on the path, though, where the sun hits the strongest during the day. That's part of why I walked over here from Elnora's driveway – I didn't want to tear up the turf. But there was no mud visible where I was standing. Unless my fire melted the snow."

Bud paused, then shook his head, and finished his thought. "No, there was still snow there when I put out the fire before I left. I know there was."

The constable wrote a few more words and said, "Thanks, Bud, this is a big help. Anything else I should pass on to the folks in charge?"

"No, that's all I've got." Bud hesitated and then added, "Well, no, there's one more thing, but I don't know how others will take it."

Charlie tilted his head. "How they take it doesn't matter."

"Well … I know you'll understand when I say that … that I might have heard the bones that night."

"Okay. Tell me more."

"I didn't know it was the bones at the time," Bud said slowly, "but given today's find, I'm pretty sure now that's what I heard. They didn't speak, at least not in words I could understand, but there was definitely a sound."

Bud fell quiet for a long moment. Then reflecting aloud, he added, "It sounded … almost sad … I guess is the closest I can get."

Finally he took in a deep breath, nodded his head, and took a step back as if to indicate he was through. Charlie nodded as well, and closed his notebook. The two men looked at each other and Charlie reached out to shake Bud's hand.

As Charlie turned to walk over to the other law enforcement officers and Bud returned to his group of friends and students, a state trooper headed toward and met Charlie. They conferred for a moment, then the trooper called Matthew Spencer over.

"Mr. Spencer," Charlie said, "this is Corporal Sanderson. He's got a couple of questions for you."

"This won't take long, Mr. Spencer. Thank you for staying around."

Matthew nodded slightly, looked down at the ground and then at Charlie. As Matt drew in a deep breath, steeling himself and trying to stand taller, Will and Sherman came to stand nearby in silent support, though far enough away so they wouldn't hear anything.

The previously-unseen red-wing blackbird flew up to the tip of a nearby cattail reed and started his territorial song again. Bud stopped, head raised slightly, to listen for a moment. As he then continued on the pathway back to the farm, a cardinal flashed by in front of him. The bird's scarlet hues were brilliant against the snowy white of the old birch tree in which he landed. Unlike the blackbird, his soft melody seemed uncertain at first, but, as Bud pulled up again and waited, the cardinal burst into his full-throated hymn to springtime for all the world to hear.

Chapter Seventeen

A Proud Little Town

It was almost six o'clock and Flora hadn't gotten any writing done. She had spent the afternoon trying to write, but construction work and traffic at the trailer to one side, a loud TV on the other, and neighborhood dogs and cats barking and yowling at every little movement and each other had made it impossible to concentrate. She was supposed to meet Will and Bud at the diner at six-thirty for their second writing session, but now she didn't have anything new to share.

As she fixed supper for the cats, Flora looked out at the bird feeders through the small window over the kitchen sink and wished, not for the first time, that she was back in Montpelier. Watching two of the neighborhood feral cats, the ones she called Tabby Cat and Smudge, spit and swipe at each other, she longed for the quiet space that had been home for almost twenty years.

Going from thirteen acres of mountain meadows and woods to a trailer park lot was, in many ways, harder for her than losing her father, for whom she had cared in his struggle with Alzheimer's Disease, for whom she had grieved every day of those ten long years. She didn't like to admit it, but in the short time she'd been here the tears for her 'little piece of heaven' were usually closer and more frequent than for her father. Especially on days like today.

Flora decided she would just tell Bud and Will what she was working on, explain the confusion of the day and

141

why she hadn't been able to write. She was sure they'd understand. Along with a critique of the idea that prompted her current work in progress, maybe they could give her some tips on how to write at such times.

Now that the outside cats had stopped scrapping and had gone elsewhere, one of the brilliant red cardinals appeared on the feeder closest to the window. Flora had read somewhere that a cardinal's presence meant that a deceased loved one had a special message to convey. *Who was here?* she wondered. *What should I pay attention to?*

She considered the cardinals as something of a compensation gift from the universe for having to come down out of the hills. Her father's land had been almost two miles up from the nearest village, too high in elevation for cardinals, though perfect for wood and hermit thrushes, scores of different warblers, and owls. None of those was here in the trailer park – at least not yet – so she was thrilled the first time she heard a cardinal's song soon after she moved in.

Now she continued to watch the single male on the feeder, waiting for the female to join him and her mate to start singing. She would be a little late meeting Bud and Will, but she couldn't bring herself to move from the kitchen window.

Finally the female appeared, perfectly camouflaged in the shadows of dusk. Flora hadn't seen her fly in. It was as if she had popped up out of the ground. The pair's soft *chips* kept them connected, one still on the feeder, the other on the ground.

Just as Flora was about to turn on a light and get ready to leave, she saw the male fly down and hop over to the female. He offered her the sunflower seed in his bill, and she took it just as gently before both cardinals flew off across the dirt road.

A moment or two later, as Flora was getting into her car, the male's song rang out into the deepening gloaming. "Thank you, brother," Flora whispered, deciding to lean back in her seat and listen even though it would make her that much later. When it became clear the serenade was over, she started up the car and added, "Thank you for the much-needed lullaby."

Gina greeted her with a laugh. "You just can't get enough of us, that you come here on your one day off?"

"The boys thought this was a good halfway point," Flora answered, standing at the counter to look around for said 'boys.' "I'm glad to see, though, I'm not the only one who's late."

"It's a good thing you all are. We were packed until a short while ago, but now, as you can see, you've got your pick of tables."

"Why so busy? Is this a special day of some kind?"

"Not that I know of." Gina filled up a mug with decaf coffee for Flora, placed it in front of her, and stayed close to say in a quiet voice, "But there were an awful lot of law enforcement types in and out all afternoon. I've no idea what happened, but something brought them all into town rather than up on the highway."

"I didn't hear any sirens …"

"No, no sirens, so no accidents. Not even any flashing lights. That's a good thing."

"Definitely," Flora quickly agreed. "I just hope Will and Bud weren't involved, whatever it was, and that they're late for another reason."

Gina glanced up, looking over Flora's shoulder when she saw headlights stream into the front windows. She turned to pick up her pad of order checks from the counter behind her. "Well, maybe we'll know more in a minute."

As soon as the bell over the door jingled and the screen door slammed, almost in unison, they knew they would have to wait a little longer when Mr. Billy shuffled in. After his obligatory flirtations with 'the most beautiful girls in town,' he sat on the stool next to Flora, who was still standing.

Billy nodded his thanks to Gina for the coffee that now waited for him, and asked, "What's going on over to Rushlow's? There's a whole bunch of state police vehicles around Elnora's house, and I saw Charlie in his car as I drove past. Is Elnora okay?"

"As far as I know, Billy, she's fine," Gina replied. "I haven't heard otherwise, anyway."

"Well, that's a relief," he said, and breathed out a long sigh.

"And now we know where all the activity has been," Flora added. "We'll find out why at some point, I suppose."

Gina and Billy looked at each other and smiled as they then looked at Flora. She looked back at them with raised eyebrows, waiting.

Gina nudged the young woman and said, "That's the first time you've used the term 'we' when talking about things going on in town."

"Yep," Billy nodded, patting her hand. "Reckon you're one of us now, don't you think, Ms. Gina?"

Flora flushed, both in embarrassment and pleasure. "Working here helps," she said quietly.

"It sure does," Gina said. "You get the good and the bad in this place. Of course, it's mostly good in this town. Every day's a new slice of life. And speaking of slices," Gina continued, reaching for napkins, and forks and plates, "who'd like some of our good maple pecan pie, eh?"

Mr. Billy looked at her. "Is it on the house?"

"Of course," Gina laughed. "We're celebrating," she said, emphasizing the 'we' with a wink at Flora.

"Well, young lady," Billy said to Flora, patting the stool next to him, "since you've now become one of us, we'll need to get you your own coffee mug."

"You mean I get to go up on the shelf, too?" she said, sitting next to the old farmer.

Billy nodded vigorously as he tucked into his pie. Before he took another bite, he said, "I hear around town that you're a writer. So I want to know when you're going to put me into a book!"

Flora caught Gina's eye as she assured Billy with a smile, "You will definitely be a character in a story, Billy. Don't you worry about that."

Every once in a while, Bud felt as if he were in something of a bubble from childhood. Something – sights, sounds, smells – would take him back to the years he grew up in the Northeast Kingdom, when he would visit his grandparents' farms or friends' woodlots and sugarbushes.

Now that he was home again from Elnora's and away from the crush of people, Bud was resting outside on his small back deck, enjoying the first evening that was warm enough to be comfortable. Before the sun had fully set, he could hear the peepers ease into their evening chorus. The longer he sat outside, the louder their collective song grew. Eventually it seemed as though the woods were going to explode from the crescendo of amphibious arias.

He thought of his grandmothers, sitting on their respective porches on such evenings, mending clothes or folding laundry in the dwindling twilight. Without fail they had to remind him, year after year, that the peepers and their vernal pools had to be 'frosted' three times before spring truly arrived.

Bud knew, then, that tonight was only the start of the warm-up, that the temperatures could – and likely would – plummet again enough for frost, and even snow was possible, but he always treasured this first moment of the spring songs. At least, he thought, the process here didn't take as long, and it started earlier, than upstate, where he'd heard there was still snow up to the windowsills this year.

As he gradually relaxed into the large Adirondack chair near two of the birdfeeders, he had a feeling he had forgotten something. When it didn't come to him right away, he thought to himself as he struggled to stay awake, "I'll have to take in the feeders tonight." If the peepers were out, it was also time for the bears to start waking up and they would be hungry. As Bud well knew, neighborhood feeders were an easy and quick source of food as the bears made their way out of hibernation and down from the hills. As much as he loved seeing the bears, he didn't want to endanger them by encouraging their presence around people and traffic.

Finally, just before it got too dark to see, Bud stirred himself, removed two birdfeeders to take into the mudroom, and fetched the flashlight to go out again for the other two. As he reached for the torch, the phone rang.

"Hey, Bud!" Will's voice echoed from his cell phone through Bud's answering machine. "You okay, man? Flora and I are waiting at the diner for you. There's a party goin' on over here!"

Damn it! That's what I forgot, Bud said to himself as he picked up the phone. "Hi, Will. Sorry I'm not there. With all that happened this afternoon, I just forgot."

Will's voice returned to normal once he heard Bud speaking. "Hell, I understand – no worries. Do you feel like coming down? We're not doing any writing tonight, as I guess you can tell from the noise ..."

"Yeah," said Bud. "It sounds like a good time," he added, listening to the spirited hullabaloo behind Will's open phone line. "What's going on?"

"Gina and Billy decided to celebrate the fact that Flora said 'we,'" Will explained with a laugh, "and it grew from there. Wait a sec, hold on. Gina's talking to me ..."

He was silent as he listened and then added, "She said to tell you there's a piece of maple pecan pie waiting for you and we'll explain when you get here."

Will couldn't see Bud's smile, but he could hear it in his friend's response. "Well, how can I resist such temptation? Tell Gina I'll be there in a few."

"Will do! All right!"

Bud could hear cheering in the background as Will signed off, and he shook his head in affectionate wonder that his friends cared so much for him. He finished storing the birdfeeders for the night, turned on a couple of lights for his return, and within fifteen minutes he was seated at the counter among his friends.

The diner was crowded for a weeknight, other townspeople overflowing to some of the tables in the front section. Along with Gina, Flora, Mr. Billy, and Will, of course, Abby, Sherman, Charlie, and even three or four state troopers were there, too. He learned the troopers had stopped in on their way back to the barracks in Shaftsbury, had been invited to join the impromptu party and, now off duty, had stayed. Cindy had come in to join Charlie and one of the troopers in a booth.

Bud hadn't really expected Elnora to be there after all the activity at her place earlier in the day, but he missed

KT's bright giggles right away. As soon as he joined Flora, Will, and Abby at their table, though, he found out from Abby that Wanda had been released and KT was staying with her overnight to help her adjust from her hospital stay.

"I'm glad Wanda's daughter hired KT," Bud said, taking his complementary maple pecan pie from Gina with a smile of appreciation. "KT is such a gem, and they get along well together."

He took a bite of the confection before him and then said, looking at Flora and Will, "I, on the other hand, am not such a good person. I completely forgot about tonight, and I haven't got any new writing to share. I apologize."

"Not to worry," Will said. "We don't have anything either. It's just been too busy, especially today."

Flora added, "And too noisy. I didn't have to deal with what you all did today – and didn't even know about it until I got here – but the noise at home was just too distracting. I'm still having a hard time getting used to the fact that there's almost no silence where I am now."

Abby touched Bud's elbow and said, "You need to take her to your special spot, Bud."

"Yes! That would be perfect," Will said. He looked at Flora and continued, "It might be hard to write there, just because it's in the woods, but you'd certainly get your fill of peace and quiet to tide you over for a while."

Flora looked at each of them in turn, her face expectant. "Oh yes, please! I really need some of that. Where is this magical place?"

"It's a small pond off a forestry road on the other side of town," Bud explained. "Almost no one goes there, except the occasional through hiker and hunters in season. The road is open only from Memorial Day to November 1st, so I go as often as I can during that time. Even just walking along the road is restful, but the little overlook at the pond itself is, as Abby said, special."

"It sounds perfect," Flora said with a soft sigh. "I would love to visit it, if you don't mind showing me."

"I don't mind at all," Bud assured her. "As soon as they open up the road, then, we'll go check it out."

As the four friends fell into a comfortable silence, Bud ate his pie slowly, almost contemplatively, as he observed all his friends and colleagues around him. It felt like everyone was letting off steam after the tensions and questions of the afternoon, enjoying each other's company as they waited for answers.

He thought, not for the first time, how glad he was to live in this proud little town, and how thankful he was for how they took care of each other.

Chapter Eighteen

Interlude

He pulled into his driveway and up to the dark house. After he turned off the ignition, Matthew sat in the car, hands still on the wheel. He stared straight ahead at the garage door but didn't reach to activate the opener. Except for the timed red blink from the security system in the car, there were no lights visible in his immediate line of sight. The closest streetlight was several houses away, and he didn't lift or turn his head to look in the mirrors at the pale lights of one or two of his neighbors' windows behind him. Because it was almost midnight, all he saw was the dim surface of the grey-painted garage door.

At first Matthew just sat in the driver's seat. Except for taking his hands from the wheel, he made no movements. He wasn't aware of any thoughts. His brain was empty and just as still as his body. After a few minutes he leaned his head back and closed his eyes.

"In a blink it's gone." Immediately Matthew's thoughts started to swirl and he remembered the Zen koan he'd read in some religious pamphlet his mother had left lying around the house. He'd wondered at the time, seven or eight years ago, if she was trying to tell him something, for soon after that she and his father had decided to move to Florida for half the year.

Thinking of his parents in Florida led to thoughts of his younger brother and sister. They had both gone to college there and liked it so much they had stayed, gotten good jobs, and, eventually, gotten married. His brother now had two young children, too. His brother and sister, together, had convinced their parents to make the move to snowbird status. The last email he'd had from his sister, youngest of the three siblings, included the news that she was pregnant and due in the early fall. Matthew wondered if their parents would bother to come back north for the summer, now that they had a third grandchild to prepare for.

His sigh was deep and long. Apparently all he was good for was looking after the house in his parents' absence and feeding his mother's birds. *Which reminds me,* he thought to himself as he opened his eyes again, *I'll have to get the bag of seed out of the car in the morning.*

Matthew finally stirred and reached up to the visor to activate the garage door opener. Once he drove the SUV into the garage, he retrieved his phone from the cubbyhole in the dashboard, and hurried into the kitchen before the light went out.   As soon as he'd done that, he remembered the case of beer he'd left in the car.

Might as well get the birdseed while I'm here. No, he decided, tomorrow was soon enough. Then he could pour the bag into the bin his mother kept in the garage so 'the critters' wouldn't get it.

Back in the kitchen, he opened up the case of beer and stowed it in the refrigerator. Already the beer was satisfyingly cold from its evening-long wait in the car as he'd driven aimlessly around Albany, Troy, the back roads of Rensselaer, Latham, Colonie, and finally back into Center Brunswick and home, and he kept one bottle out to open.

152

Spencer leaned against the island as he drained the bottle. The overhead light glared above him and seemed to ricochet off the clatter of the empty he tossed into the stainless steel sink a couple of steps in front of him. He reached into the refrigerator for another beer, twisted the top open, took a couple of big swigs, then proceeded to empty his pockets onto the island. His phone, change, keys, some lottery tickets, and a receipt for the beer all landed in a pile in the middle.

He picked up his beer, turned off the light, and went into his office. He bypassed the overhead light in favor of the small desk lamp and put the bottle down next to it as he pressed the blinking button on the answering machine. As soon as he heard his mother's message, he went out into the kitchen again and stood at the refrigerator. After a moment's thought, he opened the freezer on top and pulled out a packet of cigarettes that had been pushed to the back of the uppermost shelf.

Still in the dark, he rummaged through a couple of cabinet drawers for matches. Once he found those, he snatched up a stray saucer to use as an ashtray, strode back into the office, sat down, lit a cigarette, and pressed 'replay.'

'Hi, Mattie – This is Mom. Hope all is well there. Gotten much snow? It's nice and warm down here, of course. Listen, Dad and I have been thinking ... We're going to sell the house. There's no need for us to be in Albany anymore – except for you, all the family's gone, or down here. Right? I guess you know Linda's pregnant now, so there's another grandkid on the way, and Dad and I want to be here for good when she's born. That way we can help out. They don't know the gender yet, but I know

it's going to be a girl. Anyway, just wanted to let you know we'll be calling agents next week, so you'll need to be available to show them the house. Which means it'll need to be cleaned up. If you can't do it, there're people who do that kind of thing. You can pay them, I'm sure, and we'll reimburse you later. We want to do this as soon as possible ... So that's it from here. Everyone says hi.'

Matthew lit another cigarette, turned off the lamp, picked up his beer, and sat back in his chair with a loud sigh. "Fuck," he muttered to himself as he stood up. "Fuck, fuck, fuck!" he added aloud into the darkness, hitting the desk with a knuckled fist for good measure. He pushed his chair back hard enough to hit the wall behind him, gathered up his beer, cigarettes, and ashtray, and proceeded to march down the short hallway.

When he reached his room, which he had shared with his brother as they grew up once their sister had come along, he put his beer, et al, on the dresser to the right of the door and turned on the overhead light. Then he went to turn on the lamp on the small table between the two twin beds that still remained after all this time. He pulled out a pillow on his bed and plopped down, hands behind his head on the pillow, and glanced around the room.

Immediately Matthew got up, turned off the overhead light, finished off his beer, and took the cigarettes and saucer over to the bedside table. Another cigarette flared as he touched a lighted match to it and, sitting on the edge of the bed, one foot on the floor, the other leg drawn up beside him and bent at the knee, he studied the room in which he had spent the better part of his life.

Not much to show for a lifetime, he whispered. It's messy, he knew, but there was little clutter. *Just need to make the bed, really, and put away clothes.* Matt gave himself a quick nod. Even his mother would say that.

He finished and stubbed out his cigarette – *I'll have to get more beer and cigarettes in the morning,* he thought, opening the pack to look at the dwindling supply of tobacco – and moved over to the bookcase under the window that looked out over the side yard. The few books on the two shelves were wedged in among some of his pre-high school athletic trophies.

He decided he could bear to get rid of the trophies from his youngest years, so he pulled them out one by one. After a moment or two, he sat down on the floor, legs crossed, and went through the pile beside him. Fifteen minutes later, when he realized he was merely moving the trophies back and forth between two piles, one to keep and one to throw away, he thought he would do better to wait until tomorrow to finish and he started to place the trophies back on the two shelves.

Between the late hour and the beers, he didn't put them back in their previous places. He tried to shove a sturdier one – he'd noticed that the younger he'd been, the more plastic the trophies were – in between two taller books, but he had to remove the books to make room. After all the trophies were back in the bookcase, he looked for spots for the extra books. Finding none, he put them on top of the case. He would deal with all of that tomorrow.

Matthew got up on his knees and then to his feet. Once he was standing, he looked down and saw that the top book was his yearbook from ninth grade, his first year of high school. *Okay,* he told himself, *one quick look and then it's trash.* He took it over to the bed, lit a cigarette, and started to page through.

Oh, my God ... Face to face again with friends and teammates from so long ago, Matthew went slower and slower through the pages. When he reached the back, where the myriad teams were each grouped together, he scrutinized each photograph, looking for familiar images and memories.

The last two group photos were of his baseball and football teams. He'd made junior varsity in both, but, he remembered, he struggled to make the baseball team. He was a shoe-in for the first string non-JV pitching squad, but he wouldn't be satisfied unless he made JV. His dad had worked with him when he could, but that wasn't often because he had to work so many additional hours for the Post Office, so Matthew spent long days at school putting in extra practice time.

He found his individual photograph among the junior varsity team members and read the inscription below it. Each of the boys had been asked to provide a saying that inspired them, and Matthew's came from their head coach. Coach Jameson – Coach Jamie, they called him – had treated him to McDonald's after one particularly long, arduous workout, and they'd sat and talked for a good while after they finished their meal.

Matthew was sitting on his bed again now, the yearbook spread open on his legs, his back pillowed against the headboard. He lit another cigarette as he remembered that evening and all the practice sessions that had led up to it.

156

He knew his problem, and Coach Jamie knew he knew it. He was a good pitcher – already good enough for JV – but he couldn't connect with the bat when it was his turn at the plate. He couldn't hit the ball. Not often enough, anyway.

'Mattie, you know who Babe Ruth was, right?' Coach Jamie asked him as they gathered up their trash onto the trays. 'Well, he said something that's helped me over a hump or two and it might help you.'

'You, Coach?' Matthew said, surprised the coach needed help with anything.

'Yes, me. Babe Ruth said *Don't let the fear of striking out hold you back.* I still repeat it to myself to this day when I'm faced with something that looks or is difficult. We're only human. We have to start somewhere, right? Think about it. You're much better than you were when you were in Little League, and you're better than two years ago when you first arrived at school. The important thing is you keep improving, and that's because you work so hard. It'd be one thing if you didn't – if you didn't work so hard, I wouldn't believe in you so much, but I do believe in you. You've got it in you, I know you do. And I think if you loosen up at the plate, as loose as you are on the mound, I think you'll start to hit better.'

Don't let the fear of striking out hold you back, Matthew had said to himself from then on, every time he stood at home plate. His improvement wasn't as fast as he'd have liked – he was hoping for immediately – but he did get better with almost every practice. Even Coach Jamie could see it. When the time for JV tryouts came around, Coach had encouraged him to give it a try.

His cigarette out, Matt turned off the bedside lamp and stretched out on his side, the yearbook still open in front of him. He closed his eyes and thought of the day following tryouts. He'd been miserable through his classes as he waited anxiously for the lists to come that afternoon. As soon as he could, he made his way to the gym.

Arms crossed, Coach Jameson stood at the doorway of his office, smiling as the boys milled around the bulletin board next to him. Most of them were happy with the results they saw. For those who weren't, Coach had a word of support and an arm around their shoulder. When he saw Matthew come into the gym, he leaned back against the wall, arms crossed again. Matt looked at him for a clue, hopefully a smile, about the results, but Coach remained straight-faced.

Matthew's approach was slow and tentative. He wanted desperately to know – and he *really* should've peed first – but he didn't want to know bad news. 'Come on, Matt,' Coach had said. When he stayed where he was, Coach added, 'Remember Babe Ruth.'

Those were the first words in his mind when Matthew woke up the next morning, and he couldn't help but smile as he remembered again how relieved and excited he had been when he saw his name on the JV roster. It was down near the bottom, but Coach Jamie had leaned over to him and whispered, 'You won't be there long, Mattie. You're JV material. You know why? Because you didn't hold back.'

As soon as he got out of bed, he set aside a place in his room for things he would keep. The yearbook was the first thing he put there. His JV trophies were next. And,

158

Matthew decided, he would go to his high school reunion. Maybe he'd be lucky and Coach Jameson would be there.

Chapter Nineteen

Investments

When Matthew finally walked into his office the next day, his associates met him with a mini-barrage of apprehension. Sonia Aronson and Jacob Johnson were both on the phone at their separate desks, but as soon as Matt closed the door behind him, they tossed their phones aside and stood up in a rush.

"Where have you been?" Sonia asked, her voice a little shrill and her hands on her hips as she stood up. "We've been calling and calling … You're never this late."

Jacob looked up at the wall clock as she spoke, then added, "We had just decided to wait another half hour, until noon, before we called the police."

"Thanks for your concern," Spencer said as he continued on into his own office. Once behind his desk, he looked at his colleagues, who had followed him. "Truly. I mean that. Yesterday turned out to be pretty tough. I needed a few hours of quiet to think, so I just unplugged from everything."

As he took off his suit jacket and turned to drape it carefully over the back of the chair, Sonia and Jacob caught each other's surprised expression. Matthew Spencer had never spoken to them like that before, so quietly. And he was *never* far from his phone.

Sonia sat down in one of the two chairs in front of the desk, her dark eyebrows drawn together as she perched near the edge of the chair and waited for Matthew to sit, too.

"So what happened yesterday?" she asked with some hesitation. She wasn't sure how long her boss's contemplative reticence would last, but something told her it would help him to talk. "You seem tired," she said, as if offering him a way to start.

Spencer nodded slowly and gestured to Jacob to take the other chair. The two associates looked at each other again. This couldn't be good.

In his nervousness, Jacob blurted out, "While we were waiting for you, I talked with some new potential investors, and ..."

"No need for that anymore," Matthew said. "At least not for a while."

"*What?* What do you mean?" Sonia asked.

Matthew heaved a big sigh and sat all the way back in his chair. He started to swivel around to face the windows, either out of habit, or, Sonia thought, in an attempt to distance himself from his colleagues. But he thought better of it and turned to face them again.

"I'm glad you didn't call the police," he said. "I've had enough of them to last a good long while."

Sonia moved farther forward in her chair, and Jacob started to speak and then thought better of it. They waited silently for Matt to continue, their eyes not leaving his.

"Okay, here's what happened. You know I had a meeting yesterday with the Arlington lawyer and that guy from the private school. Well, I was late and driving too fast, so I got pulled over by the constable …"

Jacob and Sonia both shrugged their shoulders in a silent 'so what?' That wasn't unusual. There had to be more.

Matthew's wry smile acknowledged their dual gesture. "I know – so what else is new, right? That was only the start, and all that did was make me even later for the meeting. The shit started hittin' the fan when I got to the meeting and was talking with Weeks and Putnam," Matt explained. "Weeks, the attorney, got a phone call from the constable, who said that some state troopers wanted me to go up to the Rushlow property. When I got there – Weeks and Putnam went with me – I was told some bones had been unearthed in the area where we'd been back in March, and they wanted to ask me some questions."

"So is that where you've been? Jacob asked almost eagerly. "You've been in jail?"

Sonia's glance alone was enough to scold him into silence. Matt, though, knew Jacob didn't mean any harm. He was still young enough to be excited at the prospect of something new and different from the daily office business, or lack thereof.

"No, Jacob, I wasn't arrested," he said, a ghost of a smile crossing his face. "There's nothing they can arrest me for. But they didn't know that at the time. All the police knew was that we'd been on the property, and they wanted to clear up any questionable possibilities. I have to say," Spencer reflected, "they were damned nice about it all. It seemed like it took forever – they called in the medical examiner, for one thing, and had to wait for her to get there – but they're good at their jobs and were just being thorough."

He stopped speaking and stared off into the space between Sonia and Jacob, and all three of them were quiet with their own thoughts. After a moment or two, Sonia asked, "So what now, Matthew? You said we weren't to call new clients?"

"I don't know yet, to be honest. That's part of what I was thinking through last night." Matt sat up straight in his chair. "I do know we can't do anything else with Spencer Meadows until I hear back from the police, and I have no idea how long that will take." He paused and then added, "Looks like we'll have to find a new project, eh, guys?"

Jacob asked, "Do you have something in the pipeline that we can start on?"

"No, not really," Matthew said, not looking at his colleagues.

Sonia said on an indrawn breath, "So what do we do, then?"

After a moment of silence, Spencer finally looked up at Sonia and Jacob. "To be honest, I don't know. I just don't know."

Sonia stood up. "Then I suggest you take the weekend to think about it."

She moved to the doorway, turned around and looked at the two men. "I'm going home now to update my resumé and do some research. I recommend that you both do the same. Today is Thursday. If, by the time we get to work on Monday, none of us comes up with something that will employ each of us to the best of our abilities, I will tender my resignation, effective immediately."

The silence that filled the office after she closed the door was resounding. Matthew got up and looked out the window that faced the parking lot. When he saw Sonia reach her car and get in without a backward glance, his shoulders slumped. After a moment, Jacob left the office, too, softly pulling the door to behind him.

***

Abby couldn't afford to be so sleepy. Fridays were usually busy at the clinic, and today was no exception, but she had tossed and turned all night and now she was paying for it. She couldn't think why she'd been so restless – nothing hurt, she felt fine, she'd had no bad dreams that she was aware of, she wasn't wrestling with any personal problems, her bedroom wasn't too hot or too cold – but she could not fall asleep for any sustained length of time.

KT, who had plied Abby with coffee all morning in between patients, suggested the waxing full moon was to blame.

"That doesn't usually bother me," Abby mused. "In fact, I love it when the moonlight shines in through the windows."

"Did Gilda behave? Or give you enough room? I know Samson and Pudge were a bit more snuggly last night for some reason."

Abby chuckled. She liked that she and KT could share their cat experiences with each other.

"Gilda did behave, and she gave me plenty of room. In fact, she slept down at the foot of the bed for once, so that wasn't an issue." She shook her head at the thought. "It never ceases to amaze me, though, how such a tiny cat can take up so much room sometimes."

KT handed her a chart. "Your last patient for the morning," she said. "Maybe you can get a short nap before the afternoon rush. That might help you figure out what's going on."

"Good idea," Abby said. "I like the way you think, my dear. Why don't you go on and set up the answering service, then, and get your lunch? I'll close up after I'm through."

"Don't forget to set your alarm clock …"

Two and a half hours later, Abby was glad of KT's reminder. As she rolled over to turn off the beeping alarm and stretched, she knew she could have slept a few more hours, but she did feel better, more refreshed.

Before she left her private part of the house, she brewed some tea to take into the clinic with her. While the kettle was heating, she played a little with Gilda and then decided to write a group email to Will, Bud, and Sherman.

'Can we meet for a few minutes sometime this weekend?' she wrote. 'I've had an idea.'

"I like it," Will declared and looked at the others. "I'm willing to give him a call tonight if you'd all like."

"And I'll call Elnora," Abby added.

They were in her study the next afternoon. Coffee mugs, tea cups, and the crumbs of a deli lunch were spread out on the Mission-style coffee table. Gilda the black cat was curled up in her usual place on the couch, this time between Bud and Sherman. Abby and Will sat in the small wing chairs at either end of the table and sofa. The morning clouds had given way to a light rain and fog, and now they were spitting small pellets of icy graupel.

Abby got up to turn on more lamps and the illuminated pale yellow walls instantly warmed up the room. While she was up, the phone rang. Looking at the Caller ID, she announced to the others, "It's Charlie. Maybe he has some news."

"Hey, Abbs," the constable said when she answered. "I'm sorry to interrupt your Saturday afternoon, but I thought you'd like to know we've got some preliminary results from the medical examiner."

"That was fast …"

"Well, this is just the early finding, but the ME wanted to tell us right away so we can stop worrying about one thing at least. She's confirmed that the bones *are* human, but they are not recent. She still has to run another test or two, she said, to determine how long they've been there – and if they've been moved or tampered with – but for now she said there appears to be no sign of anything untoward."

"That's good news, Charlie! Thanks for letting me know. May I tell Will and Bud and Sherm?" Abby asked, turning to look at the men. "They're right here."

166

"Sure. That would help a lot. I was going to call them next, so I'll call Spencer now instead."

"Oh, I'm sure he'll be glad for the update."

"One other thing the ME said that you might be interested in. They found a small piece of what looks like pottery or possibly jewelry. That went to the forensics lab. She said she'll call with more information as soon as she can. So we have to do some more waiting, obviously, but hopefully we'll have more specifics soon."

"And hopefully more good news. Thanks so much, Charlie."

"You bet."

"Well, I think I like the sound of that," Sherman said.

Abby returned to her seat with a sigh of relief. "With good reason," she said. After she relayed all the information to the others, she added, "Charlie said he was going to call Matthew Spencer next with the preliminary news."

"That should make him feel a lot better," Sherm said, "and will be a good way to begin your conversation when you call him, Will."

"Elnora will be glad to hear the news, too," Bud added, looking at Abby. "In fact, why don't I go over there when we're through here and tell her in person? I'd like to go out to the site anyway, at least as close as I can get. There's just something out there that's calling to me."

***

Will showed up at Spencer's office about 10:30 on Monday morning. When he opened the outer office door, he found Jacob and Sonia sitting at their desks but apparently doing nothing. Their coats were laid out across their desks, as was Sonia's purse, and there were no papers visible. There was no sign of work. Neither was talking to the other. They just stared into the empty space between them. Even the phones were quiet.

"Good morning," he said, almost as a question, as he stood inside the door with his hand still on the knob behind him. He looked back and forth between the two associates. "You may not remember … I'm Will Putnam from Arlington, and I'm here to see Matt Spencer, if he's here."

Two shaking heads responded together, then Sonia said, "No, he's not here, Dr. Putnam. But I hope he gets here soon. He was supposed to make some decisions over the weekend and report back to us this morning. If he doesn't come in by 1:00, Jacob and I are ready to go elsewhere."

"Ah," Will said, glancing at their coats now in understanding. "Have you tried calling him, by any chance? I wanted to talk with him yesterday and the night before, but he never answered or returned my calls."

Jacob reached for his phone and said, "We haven't yet, but I will now, since you've come all this way."

"I'd appreciate it, thank you. I tried him again before I left Vermont, but there was still no answer."

Neither associate thought to invite him to sit down, so Will remained at the door as he waited. A moment later, Jacob shook his head again, obviously listening to a voice mail recording. "Matt," he said into the phone, "Will Putnam from Arlington is here to see you. If you're there, please pick up or call back." He paused and then added, "Sonia and I are waiting, too, by the way."

When he hung up, Jacob looked at Will and held up his hands, palms up, without saying a word. Finally Sonia asked, "Will you wait, Dr. Putnam? There's no telling if or when he'll call back."

Will was starting to feel uncomfortable, and it wasn't just with the oppressive atmosphere that was growing stronger by the minute, nor with the listless attitude of Spencer's associates. He wished Abby was here. She'd be able to tell him if he was right to be worried now, but she wasn't, so he decided to go with his gut.

"Do you mind telling me where he lives? I think I'd like to check on him. Just in case."

Sonia had been examining her manicure, but her head jerked up and she looked at Jacob first and then Will. "Do you think something's wrong?"

"I have no idea," Will said. "You know him better than I do. But I'd like to check anyway."

Jacob said, "I don't know how Matt would like your just showing up at his house …"

"I'll take responsibility for that," Will said, his tone decisive now. "You'll be in the clear."

Jacob made his own decision, too. "He lives in Center Brunswick, just off the Hoosick Road." He stopped to write down the address, then, handing him the piece of paper, said, "I think I'd like to go with you, if that's all right, Dr. Putnam. We should probably take separate cars."

"That's fine. Perhaps Ms. Aronson should stay here in case Matthew does show up or if he calls."

"I was just going to suggest that," Sonia replied. "And I'll try calling him again. If he doesn't answer this time, I'll leave a message to tell him you're coming."

She looked at Will and Jacob and said, "You should get going, then."

Twenty-five minutes later they drove up to the old ranch house on Plank Road. There was no car visible, but it could have been in the closed attached garage. As they walked up the driveway, Will noted all the blinds and drapes on this side were closed.

"Is that usual for him?" he asked Jacob.

He stopped and shook his head. "I don't know. I do know he likes to keep the house dark. He's looking after it for his parents, who are in Florida, and he thinks it keeps things safer."

Will reached the front stoop and rang the doorbell. While they waited, Jacob started to dig around in his pockets and finally came out with a house key. Without saying anything, Will rang the bell again and then, a moment later, knocked heavily on the door.

After another minute or two with no response, Jacob fitted the key into the lock. Just as he started to turn the key, they heard the garage door open and Matthew Spencer walked out. He was dressed in jeans, a flannel shirt, and lug-soled shoes, and he carried a 20-pound bag of birdseed.

"There you are!" Jacob exclaimed from the stoop, and he started down the walkway. "Where the hell have you been? We've been calling and calling! Judging from your clothes, you obviously weren't planning on going into the office today."

Will headed over to the garage to meet Spencer. He offered his hand in greeting.

"Hi, Matt. Please forgive the intrusion, but we were worried. Maybe you got Jacob's last call saying we were coming ..."

Spencer hesitated, looked at his associate, then at Will, and finally shook Will's hand in return. "No," he said quietly, "but I've had the phone off for a few days."

"Given the circumstances, that's understandable," Will nodded. "I don't blame you. I'm just glad you're okay. At least you seem to be."

Will let the intended question go unasked and then added, as he gestured for Jacob to join them, "The reason I've been calling is to give you some good news."

Matthew put the bag of seed down. "Oh? What's that?"

"Our constable, Charlie, called Dr. Abby Saturday afternoon with some early results from the medical examiner."

"Medical examiner?" Jacob practically squeaked. "Matthew, what exactly happened last week?"

"Uh oh," Will said, suitably chagrined. "I thought you might have …"

Spencer shook his head and said to Jacob, "I'll tell you shortly. First let me hear the news. I can use something good right now."

Will continued. "Well, it turns out the bones are not new. The ME doesn't know how old they are – she still needs to do some more tests – but she did confirm this was nothing recent."

"So nothing's going to happen to me?"

"That's right," Will said with a big smile. "Charlie called you Saturday afternoon, too, but obviously you didn't get his message either."

Spencer's shaky sigh was almost inaudible. "Wow … Now I wish I'd checked my phone after all. It's been a hell of a weekend," he finished, looking at Jacob as if in a silent apology.

Will gave them a moment or two and then interjected, "I also called because I have a question for you, but that will take some explanation. Now that we know you're all right, maybe we can talk on the phone tomorrow?"

"No need to wait," Matthew said, his voice stronger now. "Come inside, if you've got time. I can fill Jacob in, then we can talk more."

"That sounds good. Mr. Johnson is part of this, too."

Spencer put down the bag of birdseed on the cement floor of the garage and led the way into the house. Will chatted about the lack of snow in Center Brunswick compared to Arlington's three inches over the weekend, and Spencer answered with a distracted "We're usually about five degrees warmer, so we almost never get the snow you do."

When they entered the kitchen, the first thing Will noticed was a short stack of scratched-off lottery tickets near the edge of the countertop next to the sink, which was nearly full with empty beer bottles. The butcher block island in the middle of the room was cluttered with mail and junk mail flyers, prescription bottles, used plates and bowls, and a half-full bottle of inexpensive bourbon and a jelly glass. The only thing missing, Will thought, was an overflowing ashtray to go along with the odor of beer.

As soon as they walked into the shadowy living room, Jacob pulled out his cell phone. "I'm going to call Sonia so she'll know you're all right."

Spencer nodded and indicated Will could sit on the couch. He busied himself with clearing the coffee table of more food-laden dishes while they waited, and Will handed him the missing ashtray.

Jacob saw the exchange and looked at Spencer. "You started smoking again?" He seemed not to have paid attention to the food and drink detritus around them, but Will noticed he did go to the front window, when he finished his call, and opened the drapes without asking. Then, without waiting for his answer, Jacob took the ashtray and some of the dishes Spencer still held onto and took them into the kitchen.

Watching their interaction, Will made a decision. "Matthew, listen. Let me explain why I called you, and then I'll leave you and Mr. Johnson alone to talk about last week. You don't need me here for that. Is that all right? I won't be long."

"Sure," Spencer replied as he sank into a wide armchair with its back to the window. Jacob had just opened the window a little and stayed where he was, his arms folded.

"Okay, good. So Abby called Bud, Sherman, and me together on Saturday because she'd had an idea. We were at her house when we got the news from the ME, in fact. We all thought it was a good idea, and we'd like to see what you think about it."

Spencer seemed uncertain, turning around to look at Jacob, and then back to Will. "Okay, go ahead."

"Well," Will continued, "whatever happens with those bones at the Rushlow farm, it's clear your development is out of the picture now. At least for a good while, probably for good. In Arlington, at least. But we'd like you – and your associates, if they're interested – to act as the developer of the co-op the farmers and townspeople are forming. We'd pay you, of course. We don't know yet what we can afford, and I'm afraid it won't be nearly the amount you'd get from the condos, but we certainly don't expect you to do it for free."

"I don't understand. Why me, despite what I wanted to do to your town?" Spencer hesitated a moment, then added, "I think it's pretty obvious what people there think of me. They don't like me, and I can't blame them, really."

Jacob had come around to sit on the other end of the couch from Will and now asked him, "What do you mean, specifically, about developing the co-op?"

Will moved forward on the couch cushion, his hands folded together between his knees. "The specifics will have to be determined among the co-op members, our attorney, and, if you agree to this, you all," he began, including both Spencer and Jacob in his gaze and his words, "but we envision it as similar to what you do now, just on a much smaller scale. You'll line up supporters, arrange for advertising, meet with members, report to the Select Board and Town Meeting, maybe some grant writing. There will be other things, too, I'm sure. Essentially, though, you'll be responsible for making sure the co-op and its work will benefit its members and be an investment in and for the town."

Will sat back again and let the silence in the room draw out as Spencer and Jacob looked at each other, the floor, into space, and finally at Will once more.

Now it was Matthew's turn to sit forward in his chair. "I like the idea of investing in the town," he said quietly, "but, again, why me?"

"Since you said it, let me start by saying because you like the idea of investing in the town. We thought – and hoped – you would. And, more specifically, because we like to invest in people. Abby said she saw something in you change the other day at Rushlow's, Matthew, and she wants to give you a chance. The townspeople don't dislike you, Matt. We didn't like what you wanted to do, nor how you went about it. Granted," Will laughed, "you won't make money this way – not by a long shot – but I think you might like yourself a lot better."

After a moment or two, Spencer nodded slowly. "Doctor Abby's right. Something did change, that afternoon and since then. It's been a hell of a weekend," he said, looking at Jacob now by way of explanation. "When I got home that night, I had a phone message from my parents that they want to sell this house, so I've been dealing with that, too."

"A *lot* of changes," Will offered.

"Yeah," Matthew breathed.

"Well," Will said, slapping his knees and getting to his feet, "let me get out of here and let you think about our proposal. I'll be in touch in a day or two."

Matthew stood as well and the two men shook hands. "Thank you. I'll make a decision by then."

"Feel free to call me if you have any questions," Will said, walking in front of Spencer and Jacob back through the kitchen to the garage. He stopped at the door, turned around, and added, looking at Jacob, "Both of you. I know it's a lot to think about."

176

Chapter Twenty

Making Connections

The bright yellow daffodils that lined the pathways of the Academy campus always brought a smile to Bud's heart and, today, to his face. He always felt as if they greeted him personally with their winsome trumpets as he walked among them. Last fall he had planted a couple of dozen bulbs at his own place, but now he was looking for those he had divided and moved to other places around the school. It would take a year or two for the transplants to establish themselves, but the new shoots he was finding today were a good sign there would be even more splashes of sunshine to look forward to in springs to come.

Bud stood now, hands on his hips, and looked out across the quad from the westernmost side of campus and watched small groups of students and individuals on their way to the dining hall in the administration building, Putnam Hall. It was a beautiful morning, still cool but promising warmth later in the day. Except in a few shady patches under north-facing shrubs, the weekend's snow was gone, and Bud knew the peepers would likely sing again for the third time tonight.

As he turned toward the dining hall, he heard his cell phone chirp with an incoming text. Pulling the phone from his jacket, Bud saw the message, which also went to Abby and Sherman, was from Will. 'Just heard from Spencer. He's made his decision, wants to come meet with us ASAP. Anyone available this afternoon or tonight?'

Bud stopped to text back. 'Either OK with me. On my way to breakfast now, will you be there?'

'Yep. See you in a few,' Will replied after a moment.

By the time Bud got his meal and sat down at a table, Abby and Sherman had both responded as well. Bud put his phone next to his tray and waved when Will came into the dining room.

"Looks like we're on for this evening," the head of school said as he sat down across from Bud. "Is that okay with you?"

"That's fine. What time and where?"

"I thought we could meet at Gina's. Abby and Sherm will both be coming back from Bennington – Abby's at the hospital today and Sherm has a meeting with a client – so they'll probably be ready for an early supper. I suggested about six o'clock."

Will stopped to take a couple of bites of his Western omelet and looked around. "Where's Flora today? She's usually here for the breakfast service."

Bud shook his head. "She has the first shift on Tuesdays at the diner now, and then she'll be back here for supper."

"She's impressive, eh? Wish I had half her energy. I hope we can plan on getting together tomorrow night. I missed the writing time last week, what with all that happened."

"I hope so, too. As far as I know, it's still on." Bud finished his meal and gathered everything onto the tray.

"So how did it go yesterday with Spencer? Any idea what he's decided?"

Will picked up his coffee and sat back from the table. "I don't know what he's decided, but if I were to guess, I think he might agree to our offer. Abby was right – he did seem much different yesterday. He said he'd had a rough weekend, and from the looks of the house, that seems plenty true. I have to say, though, I didn't expect him to make a decision so soon."

"That could be a good sign."

"Agreed. We'll find out tonight." Will picked up his ringing phone, finished his coffee with a final gulp, and said, "Sorry, duty calls. See you then, my friend. Enjoy the beautiful day."

Matthew Spencer, Jacob Johnson, and Sonia Aronson were already waiting at a table for eight when everyone walked into the diner. There were only a few other local customers, all in the front room, and the new arrivals waved in their direction as they walked back to join the three associates from Albany.

Spencer stood as the four approached the table and silently shook their hands before they all sat down. Matthew, Sonia, and Jacob all had beverages, and soon the others had coffee in their personal mugs set before them.

"Before we get started," Abby said, "I have some good news to share. On my way back up here from the hospital, I got a voicemail from the ME's office. It seems the bones are much older than we anticipated. I need to call back – or somebody like Charlie does – for the specifics, but apparently the bones are *at least* 400-500 years old."

Bud sat back in his chair, a slight smile on his face, and closed his eyes. He couldn't see it, but Abby smiled, too, as she looked across at him, especially when he started to rock ever-so-gently back and forth as if he were singing to himself. The shock on the others' faces was a delight to behold as well.

"I must say, I'm stunned," Sherman Weeks said. "In a good way, of course."

"Wow," Will said. "Just ... wow."

The three associates looked at each other and then around the table. "So what does this mean?" Spencer asked, and Sonia added, "Does this change things?"

Sherman shook his head, folding his hands around his coffee mug. "It doesn't change anything as far as you're all concerned. At least not legally. Matthew still has nothing to worry about ..."

"Even more so now," Will interrupted.

"Right. It might mean more work for us, Elnora Rushlow, and the co-op – and you all, if you take us up on our offer – but that's perfectly fine."

Abby added, "It could mean more opportunities, couldn't it?"

"That's possible," Sherm answered. "Depending on what we do with this new information."

Matthew continued to look confused. "Okay, I get why I'm in the clear, especially now," he said, managing a slight grin, "since obviously I wasn't around so long ago. But I still don't understand what this all means."

"This means," Bud said, the smile still in his eyes when he opened them, "that Elnora's land was a First Nations site, maybe even Abenaki, and can never be developed."

Abby leaned across the table and patted Bud's hand in silent recognition of his personal connection to the news. As she did so, she felt a faint tingling in her own arm, and something stirred in her memory.

"How do you know that?" Spencer asked.

Will said, "As far as we know, the earliest European settlers didn't reach Vermont until the early 1600s, and they were up along the Canadian border and what are now the Champlain Islands ..."

"That was in 1609," Bud interjected, "when First Peoples introduced Samuel de Champlain to the lake that now bears his name."

"More than a little ironic, that," Will said. "And most settlers didn't come down to this area until the early 1700s," he finished. "Arlington itself wasn't established until 1761, even though there were some white people here before that."

Abby, musing aloud, said, "I suppose it's possible the bones belong to one or more of the earliest settlers. Maybe some family got lost, perhaps, or there a military scouting group or something. But, given that the location of the site overlooks the wilderness area and the river is so close by, I'm more inclined to think it's an old

Native American camp. What do you think, Bud? You know the history far better than I do."

"I agree. And not just because of my 'feelings' or intuition about the bones. If you think about it, the site faces east and one of the names of the ancient ones was 'the People of the Dawn.'"

Sherman said, "I didn't know that! How lovely. Well, that's enough evidence for me."

Jacob finally joined the conversation. "So will part of the extra work you mentioned earlier involve an archaeological excavation?"

"That's a good question," Will said. "Personally, I would like to see one – in part because I think we might be able to involve the kids from the schools in town – but I don't know. And I sure don't know how Elnora Rushlow would feel about that."

"Oh, I think she'd be fine with something like that," Sherman said. "A dig won't be permanent, for one thing. As an educator herself, I think she'd agree with you, Will."

Abby nodded. "She would love to have the kids around her again."

"At this point, though," Bud suggested, "as exciting as this is, it's still all speculation. We need to hear more from the ME, for one thing. So let's get back to why we're here, then, and hear from Matthew."

But Spencer asked, "Who determines what to do going forward?"

"The state forensics lab up in Waterbury will do the DNA tests," Abby replied, "and then, if the results warrant any follow-up, the Agency of Transportation, the Vermont Archaeological Society, and consultants from UVM – or some combination of all those folks – will arrange for excavation."

She stopped for a moment and then added, "I agree with Bud, and I apologize for hijacking our meeting with the new development. Let's get to why we're here in the first place."

"No need, Dr. Phillips," Matthew said. "I've enjoyed the history, and I'm glad about the good news."

"Please," Abby said, "it's Abby. No need for formalities at this point."

Spencer dipped his head. "Thank you, I appreciate that. Well, first let me say that I accept your offer to work with and for the co-op, and I want to explain how I reached that decision."

"More good news!" Will exclaimed. "That's wonderful!"

"I'm glad you think so, Dr. Putnam, because you're part of why I decided to accept. I remembered what you said to me the afternoon the bones were found, about how the land has changed so much between Albany and here, and the farms disappearing. I'd never paid any attention to the drive before, and I didn't think I was after that, but I must've been doing so unconsciously because your comment was the first thing I thought of after you left yesterday."

Jacob glanced at Spencer and said, "I expect your parents' decision to sell the house influenced your thinking, too."

183

"I think it probably made me pay more attention on the drive up this afternoon," Matthew agreed. "And their decision spurred a memory of an important time in my life, and someone who gave me the courage to keep trying when the odds seemed against me."

He stopped for a moment to take a sip of coffee. "And," he continued, "you're right, Dr. Putnam, there *are* too many changes from when I was in high school. In fact, the farm that belonged to one of my football teammates' family is gone. It's now a car dealership. Anyway, I wanted to take the time to drive up today and start to look around. I'd already pretty much decided to accept your offer, but I really made up my mind when I saw that." He shook his head a little. "That dealership's been there for a while, actually, but I just realized it today."

"I wondered why you got so quiet all of the sudden," Sonia told him.

"Yeah, I don't know why I never realized that about Tommy's farm before ..." Spencer looked directly at Will. "You said something yesterday about there being so many changes, and I guess that's what made it finally hit home. So I decided that if there has to be change, I want to be part of change that's *con*structive rather than *de*structive."

Looking at each of them in turn, Spencer finished. "And so I accept your kind offer."

Chapter Twenty-One

A New Story

Spring was finally settling in. The buds on the sugar maples were unfurling, popping open almost minute-by-minute in the late April sunshine. Some of the early warblers were already back again, almost invisible as they flitted about among the bright green, yellow, and pink infant leaves in the canopy above, and Bud could just barely hear the whispers of their high and busy trills.

He was torn. He wanted to be right where he was, here on his back deck, for the peepers were already starting their full-throated afternoon chorus, but he needed – and wanted – to go to Flora's home soon for their writing meet-up. She was going to tell them about the new project she had started, and he wanted to arrange a time to go to the ponds off of the forestry road. If the warblers were here, that meant the blackflies would be soon as well, and he hoped they could avoid the worst of the spring eruption of the stinging insects, so he and Flora needed to go as soon as the dirt roads were reopened. As Bud and the roads commissioner knew, that was usually soon after the shadblow trees back in the woods started to bloom. They had a couple of weeks still, but he wanted to assure Flora he hadn't forgotten his promise.

At the same time, Bud felt pulled, more than any other time, to go back to where the bones had been found. It was still too damp and dark for the three writers to meet there, which would have been his choice. Until it was time to go to Flora's, then, he roused himself and started to separate out Grandmother and Grandfather stones from a pile he had gathered over the years.

These small boulders would be heated by a daylong fire and used in the sweat lodge he hoped to have at the site on Elnora's land when he had access to it again. He hadn't told anyone yet, nor had he asked permission yet, but he could see it all as if it were taking place right now and it was hard to think of anything else. In another week or two, the herons would return to the rookery, and he wanted to be there to greet them with a special ceremony.

Forty minutes later Bud was on his way to Flora's. The evening was nice enough that he could have walked the mile and a quarter, especially now that Daylight Savings Time was in effect, but it would be fully dark when they broke up, so he decided to drive. Besides, he might stop in at the diner if there was time afterward. With so much going on lately, he hadn't had a chance to visit with Gina in a while.

Will's car was already there when Bud arrived at Flora's trailer, and so was KT's. He could hear laughter and KT's special giggle as he walked up the gravel pathway. In the background, peepers were singing from the millpond up around the curve in the road.

What a nice way to start a night of writing, Bud said to himself as he stood at the door, listening to a burst of laughter. *I wonder if KT will be joining us ...*

Through the open screen door, Flora saw him standing there and waved him inside. This was Bud's first time at Flora's, and he was struck by the feeling of positive energies the soft yellow walls created. *She and Abby must get along well,* he thought as he and the others greeted each other.

Aloud he said, "It's good to see you, KT. Do we have another writer among us, I hope?"

"No, no, no!" she exclaimed, holding up her hands as if to stop the very possibility. "I'm not a writer! If you need something built or put together, I'm your girl. Or some things medical. Words, no way."

Will shook his head. "As much as you read, that surprises me, actually."

KT laughed and said, "I just stopped in on my way home from Wanda's, and now I'll leave you all to *your* words. Flora's cats are telling me I've got two hungry felines of my own who need to be fed."

Bud jumped in as KT was almost out the door and said, "Speaking of building things, can I call you in a day or two, KT? I have a sweat lodge you can help me with, if you're interested."

"Sure, I'd love to help."

After KT left, Flora invited the men to help themselves to coffee and dessert, and then they all sat in the small but comfortable living room. They pulled out their notebooks, papers, and a book or two.

Bud kept his notebook closed at first, folded his hands together on top of the binder, and looked at Flora. "So tell us about your new project. I can't wait to hear!"

Flora's shy smile was as soft as her voice. "Now I don't know what to say," she began.

"Don't tell us too much," Will suggested quickly, "or you'll lose the creative impetus. But if you tell us your general idea, we can help later on if you need it."

She nodded and sat up straight in her chair. "Well, if it works, it will be something of a fictionalized memoir, with a little bit of fantasy thrown in. I started a story almost five years ago, when my dad and I were still up in Montpelier. I couldn't finish it because Dad went into the hospital, then a nursing home for rehab, and then, after another stint or two going from hospital to rehab, we had to move down here when he went into the Veterans Home in Bennington. All of that in about nine months. I was making good progress on it, too …"

"When did your dad die?" Bud asked gently.

"About three months after we came here."

"No wonder you couldn't finish," he said, picking up his coffee. "But maybe now you can."

"I hope so. I'll need your help, though," she said, looking at both men. "When I got the idea for a fictionalized memoir, that changed the story around more than a little bit. But I want to try this and see where it goes."

Will reached for Flora's hand and squeezed it. "We'll be glad to help however we can. That's what we're here for, to support each other. I think it sounds like a wonderful idea. Do you have a title yet?"

Now her smile was bright as she replied, "The new title is 'Grace Notes from a Trailer Park.'"

Will glanced at Bud and saw that he was looking at the plaque over Flora's desk. "'Home is where your story begins,'" he read aloud. "Your title fits right in, then."

"And," Bud added, "where your story continues." He paused and looked around the living room with interest, his eyes resting on the portrait of Emily.

"That's an amazing painting," he declared. "What a beautiful child. What is *her* story?"

"You'll meet her in the book," Flora teased. "She's the main character."

Chapter Twenty-Two

The Cycle Continues

They were waiting for him, all our relations.

***

"I talked with Mr. Spencer last night," Jeff Bedell told Abby. He had driven by, seen her in the front yard pulling up her SO(A)R lawn sign, and turned around to park in the driveway.

"Guess we don't need these anymore," Abby said when Jeff came over to her. "Thank goodness. And many thanks to you for working with the Select Board."

Now Jeff said, "That's why Mr. Spencer called. He's going to be at next week's Board meeting and asked if I wanted to be there, too."

"How thoughtful. He's really turning over a new leaf, isn't he?"

"Yeah, he told me he wants to apologize for the record, and then he's going to tell them about his decision to work for the co-op."

Still holding the faded lawn sign, Abby shook her head. "It's hard to believe how well things have come together." Looking directly at Jeff, she added with a smile,

190

"You're going to have quite the successful paper for your civics class."

"I hope so. This is all just in time, too," he said. "Our reports are due in a little less than a month."

"Have you ever given any thought about running for a seat on the Select Board, Jeff? You know the town and the people, you have a good grasp of the issues and you can see both sides ... Of course, your college plans might put that on hold for a while, but I hope it's something you'll consider for down the road. I know I'd vote for you!"

Jeff gave a little laugh at Abby's enthusiasm, but she could see from the flush on his face that he was pleased at the suggestion. His response was interrupted by the sound of a car horn and somebody yelling Abby's name as they drove past. A moment later, a compact silver-grey sedan pulled up in the driveway behind Jeff's yellow Subaru Baja and Matthew Spencer jumped out of the front passenger side.

"Dr. Abby! I'm so glad you're here," he said as he walked forward. "Hey, Jeff. Good to see you, man," he added, reaching to shake the teenager's hand. "I thought you were working today," Spencer said, turning again to Abby.

"I just started my summer Saturday hours today," she explained. "Once the warmer weather sets in, folks seem to need afternoon access less frequently, so I just work half-days on Saturdays through the summer. Except in emergencies, of course."

Spencer nodded. "Well, it's certainly a beautiful day and I'm glad you can enjoy some of it outside."

"I am, too. It's been a long winter," she replied with a smile. "What brings you to town, Matthew?"

By now, Sonia and Jacob had emerged from the car and come over to the others. Once they had all greeted each other, Spencer answered Abby. "It's so nice, we decided that we want to get to know the area better since we'll be working here now."

"That's a good idea. Are you just driving around, or do you have some particular places in mind?"

"We were just driving around …" Jacob said.

"Then we saw you and I had a thought," Spencer finished.

"Do tell."

"I wonder if you'd be available to ride with us and show us around, Dr. Abby? Maybe take us to some of your favorite places."

"If you're free, of course," Sonia quickly added.

"What a wonderful idea," Abby said. "And please," she reminded them, "it's 'Abby.' I'd love to ride with you. Thank you."

Jacob looked at Jeff. "Can you join us, Jeff? There's room for five in the car."

Jeff shook his head. "Unfortunately I've got homework I need to get to before Monday, but thank you."

"Just give me a couple of minutes to get ready," Abby said, "and I'll be right with you."

As she turned to go inside, her cell phone rang. She stopped to answer it, her face growing more and more determined the longer she listened. Finally she said into the phone, "Oh, you're on, mister. You are on."

"Everything okay?" Jeff asked.

He had never seen her face so dark as she answered, "That was Will. He called to report that he just saw a buzzard over the polo field."

"I don't understand," Sonia said. "You look like that's a bad thing."

With a furtive glance toward Abby, Jeff told them, "Everyone in town knows that Abby tries to be the first one to spot the first buzzard of spring."

"Yes," she growled. "And now – he made sure to tell me – Will is on his way to Gina's to trumpet his success. But," she paused as a sly smile re-lighted her eyes and she looked around at the others, "the herons are going to be back soon ..."

"Well, let's go look for them now," Sonia declared.

The afternoon proved to be a pleasant time. Abby directed Jacob, who was driving, along many of the routes she had explored her first time here so many years ago. As they traveled past small farmsteads, drove through the little hamlet of Chiselville and its covered bridge into East Arlington, by the elementary school, alongside the Battenkill River, swollen now with the last of the snowmelt from up north, Abby noted to herself the names and faces of the people who still lived in the same houses they had back then. She remembered, too, those who had come and gone. So many of them she had come to know first as patients, then as neighbors and friends.

Now, as the sun moved more directly into the west, she took these new friends up onto Route 7 to check out the rookery in the Lye Brook Wilderness Area a mile north. There were no herons yet, but the nests were intact atop the dead trees, waiting, and the water was high and tranquil. From the road, Abby could see fresh saplings floating near the beaver lodge.

They continued north on the highway to Exit 4 for Manchester Center, circled, and got right back onto Route 7 to head south again. When they reached the Arlington turnoff, Jacob turned right at Exit 3 and then, a couple of hundred yards farther on, Abby told him to turn right onto Warm Brook Road. Soon the road surface became dirt that had just been graded and the next mile or two was a smooth drive.

As they drove along, the car windows came down as the afternoon warmed up. Conversation was minimal but, Abby realized, the silence was a comfortable one. Sonia and Matthew, in the back seat, looked out on their respective sides and saw small, simple, well-tended houses with large expanses of emerging green grass and budding trees. Already a few bright dandelions punctuated the sunlit lawns and roadsides.

Nearly two miles farther on, the canopy of trees opened up to a wide field on the east side of the road, and Abby instructed Jacob to slow down.

"This looks familiar," he said.

"We're coming up to Rushlow's farm. I expect it looks a little different without all the snow, eh? If you're still here in the morning, by the way, I thought y'all might like to join us for a special ceremony Bud's been working on. It'll be here at dawn, so I wanted to show you how to get here."

The others' consensus was quick and eager, and Abby said, "Oh good! I have no idea what to expect – Bud's been secretive about it – but I think I can guarantee it will be like nothing you've seen before."

Early the next morning, the Albany crew picked up Abby and they drove again to Elnora's. As Jacob slowed down to approach the driveway, Abby glanced out her window at the property of Elnora's nearest neighbor. A small pond was partially visible through the greening shrubbery, and a young white birch tree grew in a clump on the slight rise just above the pond.

Jacob pulled over a little to let a car pass them, and as he did so Abby glimpsed a quick movement in the dawn shadows. On the ground at the edge of the pond, a young heron had emerged from the shelter of the cattails, her slow, precise, elegant steps leaving no ripples in the water.

Abby said nothing to the others. Instead she pointed for Jacob to follow the vehicle that had passed them a moment earlier. Other cars and small pickups were already there, forming a rapidly growing line, and others pulled in behind them.

The four in Jacob's car piled out and waited for Abby to direct them. Some of the people already there were forming up into little groups, and new arrivals joined them or continued walking toward the field above the back waters of the wilderness area. Calls of 'Hi, Abby!' or 'Hey, Doc!' or the more inclusive greeting of 'Beautiful day' surrounded them as they became part of the human stream away from the cars.

When Abby looked over at Elnora's house, she saw the widow come out onto the wide wrap-around porch and they waved to each other. She said to her companions, "I'm going to go over and speak to Elnora for a minute. I'll catch up with you in a bit."

The two women greeted each other with a hug. As they stood together, watching more people walk through Elnora's yard to the growing crowd in the back, Abby's arm rested over Elnora's shoulder.

"Whatever Bud's got planned," Abby said, "it'll be the perfect start to what looks like a beautiful day."

The older woman nodded and agreed. "It will be a nice day." She was silent for a moment more and watched the ribbons of clouds above them as they seemed to soak up the colors of the rising sun. Then she added softly, "We buried Dan last year on a day just like this."

Abby's arm tightened around Elnora's shoulders a little. "It's been a long year, hasn't it?"

"And an eventful one."

Now Abby was quiet for a moment and then said, "I was thinking about the dandelions as we came into the driveway, and what Dan told me about the goldfinches. May I come watch when they come back?"

"Of course, dear! Any time." Elnora's smile lighted up her face as she added, "Dan loved his finches at any time of year – their little chirps and cheery songs always perked him up if he was feeling low – but especially at what he called 'seed time.' Should be just two or three more weeks now, so I'll be sure to call you when the dandelion heads are close."

"Thank you. I can't wait to see them."

"As you know, they don't always come in force like they did that day, but it's always hard not to hope that they will. Now," Elnora suggested, "what do you say we join the others and see what Bud is up to?"

Will ran up to them just as they came down off the porch steps. After he greeted and hugged Elnora, he turned to Abby with a solemn, crestfallen expression on his face, his hands folded at his waist as if in supplication.

"Can I get a hug," he asked her, "or are you too mad at me?"

Elnora looked at both of her friends in surprise. "My goodness, what happened?"

Abby glanced up at Will before turning her back on him and giving an exaggerated wink to Elnora. Then she turned around again and faced Will.

Just as Will started to speak, Abby jumped in, her tone serious and hurt, and pulled a face. "He saw the first buzzard yesterday. As if that's not bad enough, he said he was going to Gina's to announce it. So now everyone knows."

Elnora followed Abby's lead and said, "Oh no, dear. That will never do."

"That's what I said."

"No, dear," Elnora said, patting Abby's arm. "I was speaking to William."

Will's broad shoulders drooped at his old teacher's remonstrance. "I'm sorry, Mrs. Rushlow. I promise I won't do it again."

"I should hope not, young man. Now apologize to Abby, too, please."

"Yes, ma'am."

Abby could have sworn Will almost shuffled his feet and she had to be careful not to look at Elnora.

He swallowed hard two or three times and soon said in a low voice, "I'm really sorry, Abbs. I can't help it that I saw the buzzard, but I certainly didn't have to gloat about it. It would've been better if I had just kept it to myself. Just so you know, though, I only told Gina. No one else knows."

"Well ..." Abby hesitated as she pretended to consider his apology. By now she and Elnora found it hard to keep their faces composed, and they still didn't dare to look at each other.

Abby let Elnora nudge her as if she too were a schoolchild. "Well," she said again, "all right, then. I accept your apology."

Will heaved a sigh of relief and actually clapped his hands. "Oh, thank you!"

"But," Abby added quickly, trying to keep her voice stern, "it's a good thing Gina's the only one you told."

"I won't tell anyone else," Will said, grabbing her hands. "I promise!"

Elnora and Abby finally broke down into their long-delayed laughter, and when they drew breath long enough to glimpse Will's nonplussed expression, they had to hold on to each other. Townspeople who passed by looked over at the threesome and smiled at the gaity that filled the air for a moment.

Will found he, too, was caught up in the women's contagious laughter, but his tentative smile was wary. "Wait, what's going on? What have I missed here?"

Catching her breath, Abby reached over and took Will's arm. "My friend, you've just been had. Of course you're forgiven. We were just pulling your leg."

Relief spread all over his face. "I guess I deserved that, didn't I?" He bent down to give Abby a quick hug, and then Elnora.

"You're a mighty good sport, Will Putnam," Elnora said.

"And because you're such a good sport," Abby added, her eyes shining, "I'll tell you that I saw a heron on the way over here!"

"That's fabulous, Abbs!" Will exclaimed.

"And also a little early, isn't it?" said Elnora.

Abby shrugged her shoulders. "I think so. It seems like it, by a week or two. This one was at a small pond a little farther down Warm Brook, though, not at the rookery. Maybe that makes a difference."

Will turned toward the back of Elnora's yard and, as if in silent consensus, the three started to make their way to join the others.

As they walked beneath the branches of the old sycamore and started spying their various friends, Abby felt something brush by her. She didn't see anything or anybody when she looked around, but something else breezed along beside her and she thought she heard the sound of faint giggling in the air. Thinking KT was nearby, she heard it again even as she saw KT with others in the crowd, standing still and quiet.

When they reached the field, they walked among the still-growing crowd, passing and greeting groups of townspeople, until they came upon Spencer, Sonia, and Jacob, alone near the small knoll above the waters of the wetlands. The rising sun slanted in just above them, and they saw Bud appear from the other side of the roped-off area that sheltered the bones. A sweat lodge, which made Abby think of a beaver lodge on land, was behind him, and a fire pit with glowing rocks.

Bud moved closer to the edge of the knoll, the crowd started to quiet down, and soon the morning songs of the red-winged blackbirds filled their ears. As the people watched, a student from the Academy emerged from the lodge with a rough-hewn wooden bowl in his hands. Together Bud and the student bent to the fire pit and, using a short but thick stick, scraped some ashes into the bowl.

By now the crowd was completely silent and the blackbirds' song reached its crescendo as the sunlight brightened the mountaintops. Now Bud had the bowl in one hand and, in the other, a large white feather and a bundle of what Abby knew to be the sacred white sage of Bud's people. He lighted the bundle of dried sage from the hot ashes in the bowl and blew on it until red sparks were visible to those closest to him. In the silence, Abby could hear, as if from a great distance, metal bracelets chiming against one another.

The teenager stood, arms outstretched. Bud moved slowly around him, using the feather to smudge him with the smoke of the sage. Those close by could hear Bud chanting softly as he directed the smoke up and down the young man's body. When he had made a full circuit, Bud handed the bowl, feather, and sage to him, and the teen reciprocated for Bud, repeating the slow ritual.

When they finished smudging each other, they bowed low again, and Bud came forward, looking out at the crowd. He bowed to them and sent the sacred smoke their way, the fragrance of the sage moving among them in a gentle breeze that stirred the young birch saplings nearby.

Was it Abby's imagination, or did some of the trees bow in response? Caught up in the ritual, she looked around and thought she saw faint translucent forms standing among the groups of people, silent and reverent. Her body started to feel as if it were buzzing from the inside out.

Bud moved now to the ground near the ropes. Arms spread wide, the bowl in one hand, feather and bundle in the other, he faced north, then west, south, and east, chanting in each direction. His low voice carried over the growing chorus of birds.

Bud stepped over the rope, moving carefully around the ground that had been dug up, and went down on his knees in the new grass. He relighted the sage, thin white wisps of smoke rising up around him in the clear, fresh air.

"You are the People of the First Light," Bud intoned as if to himself, standing up slowly and looking eastward across the water, but somehow the people closest to him could hear and some moved in closer from the back of the crowd.

"You came before us, you were the early ones. You lived, loved, and worked, played, laughed, and died on this land, near these sacred waters. Now we have come in thanks to settle you once again in your rightful place. Soon we will give your bones back to the land, back to the People."

Once again, Bud faced the four directions, turning deliberately as he sent the smoke forth, then he stretched upward to the sky and, finally, bowed low to the ground. After a moment or two, he stood up again to his full height and gazed out upon his friends gathered silently in front of him, many with their hands folded as if in prayer.

"Thanks to all of you good people," he said, holding out his hand, palm upward, "we have come here to greet the dawn together and to honor our ancestors and all our relations. Let it be forever so!"

Bud stood there for a moment longer, as if listening to something – maybe the bracelets she'd heard earlier? Abby wondered – as he looked up to the sunrise colors blooming above them. Then he turned and walked back to the sweat lodge and sat down. Slowly, and in silence, the crowd began to disperse.

Abby and her friends were among the last to leave. As they started to walk back through the field, damp with dew, they heard the steady, soft beat of a drum join the chorus of morning birdsong.

Abby stopped, as if she had forgotten something. She felt movement around her again, momentary breezes coming toward her. When she looked back, she saw that Matthew was there on the knoll, his eyes closed, listening to Bud as he drummed. As she watched, Matt handed something to Bud, but she was too far away to see what it was. *None of my business anyway*, she reminded herself.

She thought she saw six or seven other figures, too, dressed in brown and hard to see with the light behind them. They stood around Bud, swaying as if they were the cattails and reeds a few yards away.

Abby decided she needed to tell Bud soon about all that she was seeing and hearing, and to ask him if it was possible. Just then some soft singing reached her ears, and she remembered the passage she had read at the Easter Vigil.

This is no valley of dry bones, she realized. *These bones live here still, and they always will.*

She looked up and, just as the sun burst over the ridgeline, she saw a heron come into view. It was headed toward the rookery across the highway that had been surprisingly quiet all this time. Its long, graceful legs and wings beating time with the drum, the heron seemed to dip just above their heads, and then, a few wing strokes later, it landed in a nest in the tallest tree.

The first one of the year, Abby thought with a smile. She couldn't contain herself any longer. Twirling in a circle like a little girl, her arms outstretched, she called out for all to hear, "Welcome home!"

Author's Note

Arlington, Vermont is a real town. Though not chartered until 1761, it was one of the earliest settlements in the state. It became the first capital of the Vermont Republic in 1777. Located in the southwestern county of Bennington, it is a lovely little town. Everywhere you look there is history.

This much is true. Other things in *A Proud Little Town* are also true. St. James' Episcopal Church is a real church, and its ancient graveyard really is the site where Ethan Allen and other Green Mountain Boys are buried. Ethan's cousin Remember Baker was the first town clerk, and he did build the grist mill mentioned in Chapter Fourteen, and a sawmill.

Other historical figures who called Arlington home at one time or another were, as noted, Dorothy Canfield Fisher and Norman Rockwell. (Rockwell did, indeed, use some local folk as models for some of his paintings.) Grandma Moses and Robert Frost lived in neighboring towns in New York State and Vermont, respectively, and were regular visitors.

The first governor of Vermont was actually Thomas Chittenden. According to Wikipedia, he served two terms, the first from 1778-1789, then again, once Vermont had become a state, from 1790-1797. He lived in Arlington at some point, and he was a prominent member of the Green Mountain Boys.

The character William T. Putnam III is fictional through and through, as is his ancestry. Putnam Academy likewise does not exist in the real world. The Putnam name, however, is well-known in the town of Bennington and the county. There is, for example, the Putnam Building, a wing at Southwest Vermont Medical Center in Bennington. Putnam Road is nearby, and the old Putnam Hotel still graces the Four Corners intersection of Routes 7 and 9 in Bennington's downtown. It's possible, then, that there were – maybe still are – some Putnams in the Arlington area, but I don't know of any.

It's important to note, too, that Gina Frost is a fictional character. As far as I know, there is no such person. While I have made her a distant relative to Robert Frost in the book, no such relationship exists that I know of. He does still have descendants in New England, so I decided it might be possible Frost could have a distant cousin or some other descendant in Arlington, too.

On the other hand, the stone cottage retreat that's mentioned in Chapter Five is real. It's in Shaftsbury, a few minutes north of Bennington on Route 7A, just off Exit 2 on Route 7 North, and it's occasionally open to the public in the summer.

My depiction of the town meeting that starts the book is all from my imagination. Arlington does have a meeting every year, but I don't know the process there, nor where it takes place. I tried to hark back to the traditional day-long gatherings as best I could for a non-native whose only experience is through books, photographic images, newspaper and TV reports, and – of course – Norman Rockwell's iconic painting (which may or may not hang in the elementary school).

In addition to Will Putnam and Gina Frost, all other characters are fictional as well. While some of the locations are real, they are used fictionally in the book.

The one exception is Lye Brook Wildlife Management Area (WMA) and its heron rookery. Bisected by western Vermont's major north/south corridor of Route 7, the WMA is located one mile north of Exit 3. The photo on the cover shows part of the rookery in mid-summer.

It's important to note that I am not a resident of Arlington, nor do I know anyone who lives there. I have lived in Vermont for 20 years now, and I have visited and driven through Arlington fairly often, but I have no first-hand knowledge of the town, its people, or its way of *being* Arlington. I have, though, tried to be sensible of what I do know of small town life in Vermont as I crafted this novel. Any mistakes or errors are mine alone.

May 2016

Acknowledgements

More information about Cornell University's Civic Ecology program – 'a pathway for Earth stewardship in cities' – mentioned on page 59, can be found at https://civicecology.org. Google 'civic ecology: cornell' for details on a forthcoming book, a Facebook lab page, and much more.

The prayer that Bud Belanger recites in Chapter Twelve is adapted from 'An Abenaki Prayer,' a poem by Chief Edwin 'Joe' Pero, Coos (Cowasuck-Koasek) Deer Clan. This prayer can be found at the following Website www.bunnellgeneaologyhooks.citymaker.com/page/page/5 757723.htm. Many thanks to Mj Pettengill, wildcrafter, author of *Etched in Granite*, and a daughter of the Abenaki people, for her help in finding this. The translation from the Website is as follows:

" … Of the East may the Great Spirit and the Great Creator bless us and smile upon us. *Knikinik volcanda kottiwi kwahliwi Tapsiwi.*"

" … We are the children of the Dawn People … *Wobenakiak Mozmozik Odiozon.*"

The portions of the liturgy of the Great Vigil of Easter cited in Chapter Twelve come from the *Book of Common Prayer* of the Episcopal Church, pages 285-295.

Copious thanks to my partner Jim Vires for the idea that led to this novel, and for his ongoing good suggestions that made important differences as I moved from draft to draft.

And a ton of thanks to Christine Greenspan for her ever-present encouragement and excitement as she, too, accompanied me on the drafting and revision journey.

This little book wouldn't have happened without Chris and Jim. Thank you!

And a big thank you to my sister, Genna Tash, for reading the next-to-the-last draft and her reassuring words of support. She made a suggestion that made a significant and positive improvement for one of the characters, and he and I are forever in her debt. Thanks, Gen!

Congratulations to Bela Johnson, a sister alumna of Vermont College and a magical poet, who won the unofficial contest I held on my Website at www.magiclampedits.wordpress.com that used four different passages from the novel. A couple of her suggested re-worded sentences found their way into the finished manuscript, so she has officially earned a free copy of the book.

About the Author

Born in New Orleans, Louisiana, Genie made her way farther north with each move. She and her family finally realized their collective dream when they moved to Vermont in December 1995. In 2000, Genie received a BA in holistic studies from Vermont College, and in 2005, she received an MA in writing and creative studies, also from VC.

The author of poems, stories, and creative non-fiction that appeared in both print and online media, Genie is also the author of a novel, *Song of the Blessing Trees,* and two non-fiction books, *God's I AM in You: A Christian Vocation Discovery Workshop* (co-author) and *A Short Guide to Hospitable Writing.* In addition she has served as editor and/or writing mentor and companion to dozens of colleagues and clients.

Genie's writing / editing Website and blog, at www.magiclampedits.wordpress.com, includes most of her past columns and articles on grammar and self-editing. An additional feature, 'The Prompter Room,' provides regular writing prompts or thoughts based on daily quotes about writing and creativity.

A Proud Little Town is her second novel. Genie is currently at work on the second in the occasional Arlington Town series, *Grace Notes from a Trailer Park.* A chapbook of some of her poetry, *On the Wings of Seasons,* is due for publication soon.

Contact Genie at magiclampedits@gmail.com.